VANISHING WINGS

VANISHING
❧ ❧ ❧ WINGS

A Tale of Three Birds of Prey

by GRIFFING BANCROFT

Illustrated by John Hamberger

Franklin Watts, Inc. · New York 1972

Also by Griffing Bancroft
Snowy: The Story of an Egret

SBN: 531-02041-X
Copyright © 1972 by Griffing Bancroft
Library of Congress Catalog Card Number: 77-182289
Printed in the United States of America
5 4 3 2 1

And others of her generation with the hope (not too sanguine) that there will always be ospreys and eagles and falcons for them to see.

Knowest thou the ordinances of heaven? canst thou set the dominion thereof in the earth?. . .

Who hath put wisdom in the inward parts? or who hath given understanding to the heart?. . .

Doth the hawk fly by thy wisdom, and stretch her wings toward the south?

Doth the vulture mount up at thy command, and make her nest on high?

Job 38, 39.

AUTHOR'S NOTE

The setting for this book is the future, the immediate future.

Our ospreys and eagles and falcons have not yet vanished. But even the casual reader of current reports must add, not quite.

The reproductive failures of these birds and others, and the poison deaths of many forms of life are all too vividly substantiated in popular as well as scientific writings.

There are still ospreys and eagles and falcons in the United States, but there are far fewer than there were just a few years ago. Unless there are drastic, and worldwide changes in man's activities, the day of the last ones cannot be far away.

Polar bears and penguins have not yet been reported sick from pesticides but, at the extreme ends of the earth, the poison has been found in their bodies. So that day cannot be far away either.

Otherwise, everything in this book of the future is in the past. It has happened. —Griffing Bancroft, Captiva, Fla., and Lusby, Md., 1971

VANISHING WINGS

1

It was the supreme moment in Pandion's life. And he was terrified.

He was in empty space and he did not seem able to maintain himself. Fifty feet below he could see a rocky, uninviting beach toward which he was falling rapidly.

He desperately flapped his wings harder. For the last two weeks he had been exercising them regularly, but while standing in the nest. He had started using these muscles when his wings were still little more than stumps. Then, as the long wing feathers grew out, he would flap them vigorously, often jumping up a foot or two from the nest as he did so.

Now, on this early summer morning of his fifty-third day of life, these wings were being asked to sustain his body with no other support. They did not seem quite able to do it. He flapped harder and cried out:

Pilly-ate! Pilly-ate!

His mother, in the sky above him, was watching this first flight of her most venturesome offspring. She and his father had spent some time coaxing him out of the nest. Now, when she heard his frightened cry, she swooped down and flew alongside the youngster. She called out encouragement:

Kee-uuh! Kee-uuh! Kee-uuh!

Pandion looked at her and tried to imitate. He noticed that her legs and feet were pulled up tightly against her tail. He had been flying with his dangling. He pulled them up and found that this helped somewhat.

He watched the wide, powerful strokes of her wings and tried to use his in the same manner. He was doing better now, but his muscles ached from exhaustion. He simply had to rest them.

He was passing a large oak tree just back from the beach and he made for a limb. He had seen his parents land on such perches many times; his father was particularly adept at it, being able to do so with one foot while the other held a fish.

But the tricky maneuver, even with both feet, was still beyond the young bird. He stretched out his legs as he came in, but failing to secure a grasp, his talons slid over the round limb as he went on past it.

His aching wing muscles now refused to serve him further. It was all he could do just to keep his wings outstretched as he came down, clumsily, on the sand and rocks of the beach.

He glared about fiercely, his yellow eyes blazing, as though defying any enemy to take advantage of him. Even in this young helplessness there was something royal in his bearing, something that justified the ancient belief that he was descended from the reincarnation of a king.

For according to legend, when the Athenian King Pandion learned that his daughters had connived in murder, he died of grief at their disgrace, whereupon the gods turned him into a bird of prey. In this form, down through the years, he had earned the admiration of scientists and laymen alike. To the former he was *Pandion haliaeetus*, a sea eagle, the only member of the worldwide family *pandionidae*. To the ordinary man he was the osprey, or fish hawk.

Of all the many birds of prey in the world, he was the most friendly to man. And only man would be able to drive him from the earth.

Pandion stared up at the nest he had left. It seemed so far away, fifty feet above, a bulky mass of limbs and twigs at the very top of a nearly dead pine tree. Would he ever be able to get back to it?

He could see his brother and sister, standing on its edge, trying to work up the courage to do what he had done—fly out into space. Perhaps the sight of his failure, his ignominious crash landing, was inhibiting them.

Both his parents were now circling a few feet above him. They were calling out, urging him to get off the beach, to return to the nest.

Another old osprey was also flying above him, a visitor whose curiosity had led him to come over and see what all the noise and activity was about. He had a nest that Pandion could see, only a hundred feet along the beach.

For times were good and there were quite a few ospreys living and nesting in this Chesapeake Bay area. Human habitations were increasing rapidly, it was true, but the presence of these large earth-creatures did not bother the ospreys as much as it did other raptors.

Nor were the ospreys as fiercely territorial as most other birds of prey. As long as fish were plentiful in nearby waters they seemed willing to share and would nest quite close together, sometimes even in small colonies.

[5]

So, Pandion's parents paid scant attention to the neighbor. They were accustomed to such visitations and often flew over to see what their fellows were up to. The intruder soon left anyway, to go fishing for food for his own youngsters.

The elder ospreys, meanwhile, were increasing their anxious cries. Thus encouraged, young Pandion tried his wings once more. He found that the muscles, while stiff and sore, would respond at least after a fashion. There was nothing wrong with his legs, so he ran along the beach, flapping his wings, and finally managed to take off.

He circled around, still beating his wings rather uncertainly, but he was slowly learning the lessons of flight. His mother now came over beside him and led him inland, away from the water. Here Pandion would learn one of his most important lessons.

The climbing sun was beating down, warming the earth more than the water and warming the open spaces of the earth more than those covered by trees or other vegetation. The heated, lighter air rose up from these spaces in warm drafts, or thermals.

Pandion's mother quickly found one of these and led him into it. The youngster felt himself being buoyed upward. Imitating his parent, he circled about closely, keeping himself in the updraft, and soon he found he was a little above the nest. He swooped down into it, landing still a little clumsily on the edge.

At just about this time Pandion heard his father's cry: *Tew! Tew! Tew!* This meant food, and sure enough the old bird was approaching with a headless two-pound catfish in his talons. As he often did, the father had stopped to decapitate his prey and consume the head himself before bringing the remainder home for his family.

After all his activity the young bird was ravenous. So, when the father dropped the body of the fish into the nest, Pandion was the first to seize it with a talon and, with his beak, he started tearing off the most succulent pieces.

His siblings soon joined in the feast. While at times when they were younger they had fought each other for first helpings, the young ospreys usually got along quite amicably, share and share alike, with less squabbling than occurs in the nests of most birds of prey. Anyway, food was plentiful and their father was a good provider. There was enough for all.

The next two weeks were wonderful for Pandion. During that time, with surprising rapidity, he became adept at flying and hunting.

At eight weeks of age he was full sized, almost two feet from beak to tail with a wingspread of four and a half feet. He was now fully feathered and except that his plumage tended to be a little darker in coloring, looked almost exactly like the older birds of his species.

His head was almost entirely white except for dark streaks than ran back from his hooked beak beyond his eyes. His back and wings were brownish black, and his tail was barred with lines alternately light and dark. His undersides, however, were almost pure white, much lighter than the feathering of other hawks.

After his first, rather inglorious venture into space, he and his brother and sister began flying every day. Each time they would go a little farther and stay away from the nest a little longer. They always returned before dark, however, and continued to get most of their food from their father. The food consisted almost exclusively of fish of various kinds and sizes, although on rare occasions the older bird would bring home a frog, and once a lizard.

The young birds were playful, but the play served an essential purpose. They quickly learned to seek out and find the thermals and ride up hundreds of feet. From these heights they would swoop downward at dizzying speeds and sometimes with looping backward flights would perform somersaults in the air.

They were gaining both the strength and skill that would be needed in their hunting and travels. It was not easy. For all hawks, the first month out of the nest is the critical time. The arts of survival must be learned then or they probably never would be.

Learning to secure food was the most difficult lesson, for fish also have arts of survival. They are quick to sense either a shadow on the water or some other sign of danger from above. With amazing speed an alarmed fish can turn and dodge, or with erratic hard-to-follow motions it can plunge out of sight into the depths.

Unless they could be found forced to the surface by enemies below, trapped in shallow water, wounded, or in some such handicapped condition, which happened only rarely, it took the utmost skill and patience to catch fish.

This skill Pandion now had to master. Hunting lessons started as soon as the youngsters were strong enough to stay in the air an hour or two without tiring. On his first actual lesson, Pandion followed his father while his brother and sister went off with their mother.

The male parent led him along the edges of the inlet off Chesapeake Bay where their nest was located. At the very outset, Pandion would learn to do most of his hunting over shallow water, near shore, or over bars and mud flats. It was usually fruitless to search over waters deep enough to give the fish too much room to maneuver.

At first the youngster simply watched his parent. The old bird soared slowly along. Sometimes he would do this as much as a hundred feet above the water but usually, as now, he maintained an altitude of some thirty feet.

His wings were rather narrow with a definite crook in the middle quite unlike other hawks. This gave his outer wing more mobility with which to soar and hover over water. For here, where he hunted, unless he was extremely close to shore, there were seldom the warm supporting thermal currents thrown up by the heat of the ground that were such a boon to the vultures and soaring hawks who hunted over land.

On this first lesson Pandion flew a few feet back from his father. Suddenly the old bird stopped in mid-flight, using his wings to hover. Pandion braked his own flight just in time and looked down. Barely visible was the silhouette of a fish under the water. Instead of coming up closer to the surface, however, the fish sank deeper. The old osprey resumed his soaring.

Suddenly he peeled over sideways, his wings nearly closed. He plummeted into the water with a great splash and practically disappeared. Then up he came with a one-pound blue-fish struggling in his talons.

Thus laden, the old osprey paused in the air a few feet above the water and vigorously shook himself, getting most of the wetness off his feathers. He then flew to a treetop where, holding the still-struggling fish with one talon and starting with the eyes and head, he leisurely pulled off edible pieces with his beak and started eating.

Pandion watched him hungrily. He started soaring slowly over the water near the shore as he had seen his father do. It was not long before he caught sight of a catfish in the shallow water.

Down went Pandion. Some essentials of his hunting came to him automatically. Because of the refraction of light rays, a "bending" when they enter water, an object beneath the surface is not quite where it would seem to be if it were out of the water. Pandion did not have to learn to compensate for this. His eyes made an automatic adjustment. In addition, just before he struck the water, without consciousness on his part, his legs shot forward, ready to seize his prey.

He was also endowed with certain physical attributes to help him in securing food. Most birds, including hawks, have three toes forward and one behind. Pandion, however, like a true sea eagle, had developed an outer toe that could be shifted back or front, somewhat like the human thumb. As he struck for his target now, this toe went back. With two talons forward and two in the rear he could get a much more secure hold on his slippery prey. In addition, Pandion's talons were long, narrow, sharply curved for better grasping, and had spongy adherent pads on the bottom of his toes to make it even more difficult for a wet and squirming fish to work himself free of the deadly grip.

But all such endowments are worthless unless one knows how to use them. Pandion simply misjudged his dive. The fish easily eluded him and his eager talons closed on empty water.

Frustrated, the youngster rose and paused to shake the water out of his plumage as he had seen his father do. In this drying process nature also aided him. He had a vastly enlarged uropygial, or oil gland, at the base of his tail. In preening, which he had done ever since his feathers started sprouting, he used the oil from this gland to keep his feathers constantly waterproofed.

By the time Pandion had made his first—and unsuccessful —dive, his father had finished his meal and rejoined him. The hungry young bird now kept close to his father, emitting the begging calls he had used in the nest: *Pseek! Pseek! Pseek!*

Soon the father made another dive and again came up with a fish. This time, after rising from the water and shaking himself, the old bird soared upward, well above his son. From this height he let the squirming fish fall.

Pandion swooped after it but missed. The fish fell into the water and the young osprey instantly plunged down after it. This time, because the fish was wounded and shaken by his harrowing experience, and therefore slow to move, Pandion successfully seized his first prey.

Soon thereafter Pandion started catching fish on his own and with each successful hunt he became a little more skilled. He

was about to learn, however, that just catching a fish was not always enough. He could have trouble keeping it.

So far in his short life, Pandion had paid little attention to other creatures. In the distance he had seen men and other mammals and more often other birds. He had had, of course, a close association with his parents and nest mates and had often seen neighboring ospreys.

Only idly had he watched the active sandpipers and other shorebirds running along the beach below him and the gulls and different ducks out in the deeper water. A pair of house wrens had made a home in the lower part of the bulky nest where Pandion had grown up and were now feeding their own youngsters there, but none of the ospreys paid any attention to the coming and going of these tiny birds.

Several times since leaving the nest Pandion had been chased and dived at by a pair of pugnacious kingbirds when he had passed close to their nest. Although many times bigger than these flycatchers, and armed with his formidible talons, Pandion always fled them rather than fight.

Somehow he sensed that they were in the right, that he was the trespasser onto their territory. They could not hurt him. He had no desire to eat a bird and would not unless extremely hungry. So he simply flew away. Nature seldom condones the waste of energy on fruitless encounters.

❧ 2 ❧

Some quarter of a mile up the inlet from Pandion's nest and a hundred yards back from the water, a huge bird was perched near the top of a tall pine tree.

He was larger than the osprey, two and a half feet from beak to toes with a wingspread of seven feet. His gleaming white head and tail, in sharp contrast to his dark, brownish body and wings, proclaimed him his country's national bird, an adult at least four years old.

He was known to scientists as *Haliaeetus leucocephalus*, or white-headed sea eagle, but familiar to most as the American, or bald eagle. We will call him Baldy.

He had been sitting on the lofty pine limb for some time. He had little to do. He and his mate had raised one youngster that year. This was average. As usual, they had started with two eggs taking turns incubating for five weeks and had hatched two youngsters.

But one, the female, hatched first. She was bigger and stronger than the male anyway—in all the hawk group the females average larger than the males—so she got most of the food and her baby brother starved.

Now, in midsummer, the parent eagles should have been

feeding and caring for this surviving daughter and teaching her the finer arts of catching, stealing, and scavenging prey. They did not know it, of course, but this was the last youngster they would ever be able to raise, and now even she was no longer with them.

During their first three or four years bald eagles have plain brownish plumage with no distinguishing white head and tail. Their daughter had made only a few trial flights out of the nest before she was shot and killed by a misguided farmer. He was a man misguided on two counts.

First he had mistaken a brownish young eagle for a soaring hawk. And, second, he believed that these hawks were a threat to his poultry and livestock. Here he was also mistaken. For these hawks were instrumental in controlling the greater menaces to poultry and livestock like rats, skunks, and other mammals and snakes.

So, Baldy's bereavement being the price of human error, he was perched on a treetop with nothing to do save feed himself which, in the warm summer weather, took only part of his time.

At first, after losing their only remaining offspring, he and his mate had continued hunting and scavenging together and coming back to the nest each night as they would have done during the long process of teaching their youngster to survive on her own. They were puzzled more than anything else by her absence.

After a week or so, however, Baldy and his mate had drifted apart, each hunting alone. They would not be far apart and in any event would rejoin each other at the nesting site early the next spring provided they both survived the winter. For eagles mate for life and form a new pair bond only if one of them is lost.

From his treetop Baldy could look out over a long stretch of shoreline along the inlet. His eyes were concentrating now on Pandion as the young osprey soared slowly over the shallows searching for prey.

Baldy was a bird for whom evolution had not quite caught up with habit and behavior. Somewhere along the line his ancestors had acquired a taste for fish and about three quarters of his food was fish of some kind or other.

But he was not a true sea eagle, not equipped as Pandion was to catch hale and lively fish. He did not have the reversible toe, the adherent pads, or the sharply curved talons that would aid him in hanging onto a slippery, struggling fish. He also lacked the large oil gland that would permit him to waterproof his feathers so he could get wet with impunity while diving for fish. And it had taken him a long time as a youngster to learn to allow for the refraction of light in locating objects under the surface of the water. This adjustment did not come automatically as it did for Pandion.

Now and then, if a fish were especially unwary or kept on the surface by enemies below or somehow trapped in shoals, Baldy would catch a healthy one. Otherwise, perforce, he sought out the wounded or crippled or sick fish in the shallows, or he scavenged for dead things. Or he robbed. That is why he was now watching the young osprey so carefully.

Pandion was hunting entirely on his own. Neither parent

osprey was anywhere in sight, for the youngster was now quite proficient.

As he soared slowly along, about forty feet above the water, his eyes suddenly caught sight of a shadowy silhouette just below the surface. He braked his forward motion and hovered a moment. The shadow did not go deeper. Down came Pandion, wings open just enough so he could use them and his tail to shift course if the prey should dodge.

The depth of the victim had been properly judged and the speed of the dive adjusted accordingly and allowance had been made for the refraction in the water. The talons came forward eagerly as Pandion hit the surface and went partially under and he had the satisfaction of feeling them bite into living, struggling flesh.

He had risen, shaken himself free of most of the wetness, and was headed for a perch along the shore to have his meal when he realized he was not alone.

Baldy had left his perch as he saw the osprey rise with a fish. He was well above the intended victim and diving rapidly toward him when Pandion caught sight of his shadow in the water. At that point the eagle started screaming, although it was as much a cackle as a scream.

Cak! Cak! Cak!

The larger bird hoped this might frighten the osprey, convince him of the hopelessness of his cause, and so persuade him to drop the fish with a minimum of fuss.

Pandion, however, was too young to have learned that discretion may sometimes be the better part of valor. He would not give in so easily.

His only hope was to get above his enemy. He dodged and tried to rise at the same time. He was answering the eagle with his alarm call:

Chee-eep! Chee-eep! Chee-eep!

By now the eagle was almost upon him. Pandion squirmed aside, but badly hindered by the weight of the fish he was carrying, it became apparent that he had no chance. Reluctantly he released his prey.

Swerving by the smaller bird, the eagle went on down and caught the prize in the air just before it hit the safety of the water.

But the struggle was not yet over. The activity and the calls had attracted Pandion's mother. He saw her above him now, screaming and diving at the eagle.

And now it was the larger bird who was hampered by carrying the fish. Pandion, free of this handicap, was eager to join the fray. Both he and his mother started diving at the eagle. The robber twisted and turned. The older osprey struck him a swerving blow that took some feathers off his back.

At that point Baldy decided he had had enough. He released his stolen meal. Both ospreys had by then veered and were heading upward. The fish fell into the water before anyone could catch him. He had just enough life left to struggle down out of sight. Wounded, he would soon fall prey to one of his many enemies lurking below, but none of the birds would make a meal of him.

Pandion watched the eagle soar off and resumed his hunting. He would have more encounters with this larger bird and some lessons had been learned. Alone, and hampered by a

fish in his talons, he had no chance against the eagle. He might as well yield his prey at once and save his energy to catch another.

His rebuff by the two ospreys was not the only indignity suffered by Baldy that day.

Still hungry after the loss of the stolen fish, the eagle flew on along the shoreline looking for almost any kind of animal matter that might have been washed up by the tide.

He wisely gave a wide berth to the neighboring osprey nest. Bald eagles had been known to seize and eat a fledgling out of such nests if one were found unguarded, so he was not welcome in nesting territories. If he came too close, angry parent ospreys would be sure to come out to harass him and Baldy had already had all of that he wanted for the time being.

Two or three miles farther on, the beach narrowed where some cliffs rose behind it. Concentrating on his search for food, Baldy did not realize that he was coming under the scrutiny of some farseeing eyes.

They belonged to a bird only half his size, a bird known to ornithologists as *Falco peregrinus,* or wandering falcon. And, indeed, his wide-ranging peregrinations had carried his species, like Pandion's, around the world.

He was perched on a ledge of the cliff where he and his mate had raised, or almost raised, two youngsters. As in the case of Baldy, the falcon's offspring, too, had fallen prey to man.

Perry, as we shall call him, had nested for several years on this cliff ledge overlooking the inlet and the bay. For the last two years he had attracted to this aerie the same mate, as she, like him, had a compulsion to return to the same territory each spring.

This year as usual she had laid four eggs but, as a harbinger of things to come, two of them were sterile and failed to hatch. The parents brooded and fed the two hatchlings until feathers had replaced the grayish white down and the youngsters began running about the ledge, exercising leg and wing muscles.

Then, when they were four weeks old, about a week before the time when they would be attempting their first flights, tragedy struck. It came in the form of a man who appeared at the top of the cliff. Alarmed, the parent falcons screamed and dived at the intruder, hoping to frighten him away.

But the man persisted. He lowered a rope ladder over the cliff and, with gunnysack in hand, climbed down to the nesting ledge. The two youngsters cowered back against the cliff as far from him as they could get. They hissed and struck at him with their beaks. The parents screamed even louder and dived even closer.

It was all in vain. The two babies were seized and stuffed into the sack. The man climbed back to the top of the cliff, rolled up his ladder, and strode away. He was an illegal dealer supplying young birds, at a price, to falconers.

Perry's youngsters would now become trained performers. Through the centuries their ancestors had been subject to this form of bondage by kings and commoners alike and men today still delight in watching these formidible creatures pursue and strike down other birds.

Perry was a killer and eater of birds, and was superbly equipped by nature for doing so. His long, narrow wings gave him a speed of flight that was unsurpassed. His yellow feet and long talons, which could be used to club or to seize, were huge. In fact, the early artist-ornithologist, John J. Audubon, had called him the "great-footed hawk" and he was later known as the duck hawk and, more recently and more properly, the peregrine falcon.

Perry's large brown eyes, set slightly far apart, gave him a sight far superior to that of more earthbound creatures. If humans had eyes as large in proportion to their size as his they would measure a full three inches in diameter, and would occupy most of the space between the nose, mouth, and ear.

Perry's streamlined body was mostly bluish gray flecked with white on top, much lighter underneath, and with a black cap over his eyes and black lines extending through and below his eyes. This darkness around the eyes helped shield this predator from the glare of the sun if he was forced to pursue his prey toward it. But to some extent nature here outdid herself, for Perry usually so maneuvered as to be between his quarry and the sun.

Although his nesting scrape, a bare indentation in the sandy dirt of the ledge, was now empty and his mate had drifted away, Perry, the male falcon or *tiercel*, was still defending this breeding territory. He perched silently, watching Baldy's approach until he decided the eagle had come too close.

Perry then launched himself almost straight upward until

he was a hundred feet above the larger bird. Folding his long pointed wings and clenching his big yellow feet he started his downward dive, or "stoop," as the maneuver is called. In silence he fell toward the eagle at tremendous speed. Halfway to his target, the falcon screamed:

Kaa-aaa-aak! Kaa-aaa-aak!

Baldy tried to dodge with a quick turn but the falcon was quicker and continued toward him. At exactly the correct moment, just as it appeared Perry would strike him, the larger bird rolled over on his back and presented his powerful talons. Perry veered off just in time.

Seeming even to increase his speed the falcon executed a wide arc and climbed again. Down he came in another dive and again, with precise timing, the eagle rolled over. Literally flying circles around the intruder, Perry attacked again, and again missed the eagle's talons by inches.

The winner of this encounter would never be determined, for soon the eagle had proceeded far enough up the beach to be out of the falcon's territory. Satisfied, Perry returned to his empty cliff. Territorial matters are usually settled without physical harm to the combatants.

Perry was restless. It was unnatural for him to be alone at this time of year. He should have had a family to care for, young to feed and train. If his nest had been robbed earlier, with eggs instead of nearly grown young, he and his mate would have had a second setting. But the tragedy had come too late in the season for a second try, yet too early for him to set out on his autumnal wanderings.

The compulsion to defend the breeding territory had

[23]

stayed with him even when the need for it had gone. But after his encounter with the eagle, the compulsion began to subside. The time for movement arrived.

Leaving the ledge, Perry flew a little inland and then started down the inlet. He was hungry and this way he could keep the trees along the edge of the water between himself and possible prey. Surprise was always a help in his attacks.

He was looking for a bird flying alone out in the open. This was his normal quarry. And the first bird he saw in the air was Pandion, as the young osprey was following his usual hunting routine soaring slowly over the shallow water.

The falcon did not ordinarily prey on fellow hawks. But he was by nature playful. The sight of almost any bird in the air might stimulate him into action. He often made stoops for play as well as for predation. In the past he had chased gulls and terns along the beaches, not with any intent to kill, but just for amusement. And as a youngster he had often pursued insects only to have these tiny creatures escape between his talons.

All this did serve a purpose, as practice feints or warm-ups before engaging in serious hunting.

So now he left his tree cover and again headed straight upward. He was a tiny speck in the sky when he folded his wings close to his body and raced downward. These stoops were exhilarating, whether for sport or with serious intent to kill. He was racing toward the osprey at two hundred miles an hour. Even at this tremendous speed, Perry was able to breathe normally, as nature had endowed him with ridges along his nostrils to break the current of the air.

Pandion, still soaring slowly over the shoreline, suddenly

became conscious that he was about to be molested again. He looked up and saw the black dot in the sky racing toward him. With no fish in his talons he was able to take counteraction.

With precise timing, as the eagle had done before, Pandion rolled over just as the falcon arrived, presenting his talons to this new menace. Perry easily veered off, circled back up, and made another dive. After this rebuff, and being properly warmed up for more serious endeavors, the falcon flew over to perch near the top of an oak tree.

Through concealing leaves he began keeping watch over a small flock of lesser scaup ducks that were feeding in the shallow water near the shore. Sooner or later one or more of these diving ducks would attempt flight. All that was needed was patience. If Perry showed himself too openly they would probably seek safety in diving rather than in flight.

Pandion, a little shaken by what had seemed to him an unfriendly attack by the falcon, also flew to a perch ashore. If not as playful as the falcon, the osprey was inclined to be more curious. He had fed himself quite recently and was content to sit and watch the proceedings.

The two birds remained on their separate perches for an hour, Pandion preening his feathers, Perry closely watching his hoped-for prey. All unaware of the eyes upon them, the scaups, or blue bills as they are also called, decided to try elsewhere for the tiny fish upon which they wanted to feed.

As they rose, paddling along the water and into the air, Perry left his concealed perch. The last duck to take off remained somewhat behind the others in flight so the falcon fixed him as a target.

The lesser scaup is a small, fast-flying duck, but Perry, after gaining some altitude, stooped down upon the flock as though it were motionless in the air. With his big clenched foot he struck the rear duck a stunning blow. Unconscious, his victim shot forward and downward. Perry, scarcely slowing his dive, turned half over and seized his prey.

He carried his lifeless victim to the beach where, with the notched beak that falcons possess, he quickly broke the duck's neck. Then, lest some robber, like Baldy the eagle, spot his prize, Perry spread out his wings to hide the duck.

Behind this mantle, holding his prey in one talon, he began carefully to pluck the breast of the duck with his beak, letting the feathers float off in the wind. Finally he tore off and ate the still-warm flesh. Unless very hungry, Perry would eat only the choicest parts of his prey. So now, his meal finished, he left the remnants for some vultures who had already started to circle overhead, and flew off toward the northern end of Chesapeake Bay.

Pandion, who had remained on his perch during all this, was seized by a sudden impulse. The young osprey and his parents had now severed the family bonds. Pandion was lonely. He flew up, following the falcon.

Perry headed along the shore and Pandion followed for several miles, always keeping some distance between them. But when they neared the head of the bay, Perry turned and proceeded over the land.

Lonely or not, the osprey would not leave the water where his food was. He selected a perch on the top of a dead pine and watched the falcon, a disappearing spot in the sky.

3

Perry had no particular objective. He was just living up to his name and wandering.

After leaving the bay he flew northeast over a long stretch of open country. The monotony was broken only by a few scattered clumps of trees and shrubs that were mostly around houses or other evidences of human habitation.

He would get over it in time, but now he would not go near a man. The kidnapping of his youngsters still fresh in his memory had marked this creature an enemy to be avoided.

Now, as he soared over what seemed to be an endless expanse of low-growing greenery, he amused himself by gaining altitude and stooping down on a small flock of tree swallows causing the little birds to scatter in panic.

After a little of this he grew tired, but here he could find no place that seemed safe for perching and resting. He flew on until he sighted a small clump of trees and bushes far enough away from men to suit him. Looking carefully about, he came down and landed on a limb near the top of the tallest tree.

Somehow he sensed that there was something wrong, something unnatural about his surroundings, for except for the small, isolated arboreal island where he was perched there was none of the natural variety of vegetation that had constituted the hunting grounds of his ancestors.

Everything looked the same. He could see no other wooded areas where he might find concealment while waiting for prey. Nor was there brush or other cover where the prey might seek to elude him. It is not surprising that he felt disturbed. Once this land had had all the natural variety that he missed. There had been trees of many different kinds, shrubs, weeds, flowers, open meadows, and brush-covered areas.

This variety of plant life had at that time attracted a variety of animal life to shelter in it or feed upon it. Many kinds of herbivorous insects, birds, mammals, and other vegetable-eating creatures took advantage of the environment. They, in turn, had attracted a similar variety of animal eaters to prey on them and on each other, insect-eating insects and spiders, carnivorous birds, mammals, and reptiles.

It had been, through the ages, a balanced, stable community, its very variety a safeguard against a population explosion, against domination by a single species.

Now it was different. Man, the earth changer, had altered this delicate balance. Man himself, like other omnivores, feeds on a variety of animal prey and vegetable matter. Alone among the earth's creatures, he is able to effect drastic changes in his environment. And man has discovered the efficiency of setting aside large areas for the production of a single item of his diet in a place where that item will prosper best and through a system of exchange to trade this for other things he desires.

What Perry was looking at was a farm planted with corn.

Virtually all other plant life had been eliminated; there was only an endless sea of half-grown cornstalks that were some fifteen inches high.

This was "monoculture," the use of land for the growing of a single crop. It was, presumably, a boon to man and assuredly was a boon to corn eaters and to predators who fed on corn eaters. In the specialized galaxy of animal life, almost all others, prey and predator alike, had either died off or moved elsewhere.

The variety was gone and with it had gone the stability essential to a balanced ecological community. There was a price to pay for this.

With variations, this price was being exacted almost everywhere that men grew crops. The reckoning in this particular place had started that spring, in the same little clump of trees and bushes atop which Perry was now perched.

Tiny eggs, deposited in the bark of the trees and the stems of the plants the previous fall, had come to life. Breaking out of them, as the spring warmth spread over the land, were a multitude of soft-bodied greenish creatures called corn leaf aphids.

They immediately started attacking tender leaves and plant stems, sucking out the juices with spearlike mouth parts. And almost at once they were set upon by several predators, chief of which were the larvae of the lacewing fly, tiny creatures that looked like a cross between a miniature lizard and a worm.

These fierce predators were equipped with piercing jaws with which they could impale an aphid, lift him into the air and drink out his vital juices, shaking him from side to side to extract the last drop and then tossing aside the empty husk to seize another.

There were a few other animal eaters attracted by the aphids. The larvae of ladybugs, which simply grabbed their victims and chewed them up, spitting aside the indigestible parts, were another kind of predator. And while their progeny were feasting thus, flying adult lacewing flies and ladybugs were also preying on the aphids.

Now and then a small chalcid fly would land on the back of an aphid and with a needle-sharp oviposter place an egg inside the aphid's body. When this egg hatched, the larvae would eat out the inside of the unfortunate victim.

Ants also joined the party, some of them eating aphids and some feeding on the milklike excreta of the plant eaters.

Things might have looked pretty dark for the aphids, but against it all they had an overwhelming defense: number and prolificacy. All of these aphids were females. While they had been hatched from fertilized eggs laid the previous fall, they were now able, parthogenetically—without the help of a male—to bear living young. In fact, they were producing a new generation, still all females, about every ten minutes, which was a little faster than their enemies could destroy them.

So far this little drama had been played out in the clump of varied vegetation where the aphid eggs had been laid. Here, due to the limited amount of tender greenery for food and the voraciousness of the predators, the number of aphids began to decrease.

Under these conditions a balance would have been struck,

the population controlled. At summer's end a few male aphids would be produced, fertilized eggs laid, and the adults would die off leaving their seed for a replay the following spring. But now the conditions that had for so long assured this control had been changed.

As some of the aphids reached full maturity they acquired wings. Off they flew to search for food elsewhere. And then they entered the field of growing corn.

Here was an ocean of food that was almost as unlimited as the aphids' ability to eat it and reproduce. The predators would catch up with them, of course, and would increase as the aphids increased. But, as long as the food held out, the predators could not reproduce quite as quickly as the aphids. A population explosion was inevitable.

Perry, himself a predator, was still on his perch in the tree because his prey, birds, were also attracted to the area. Some came to eat the aphids, some to eat the predators that ate the aphids, and some to do both.

Most of the birds were small, chickadees and warblers, too small to interest Perry unless he was hungrier than he felt now. Also, these small birds were staying close to the ground, ready to duck into the corn cover at the first sign of danger. But some larger birds were attracted, mainly flickers who were after the ants that were following the aphids. The flicker is a large, ten-inch woodpecker, who above all else delights in feasting on ants. And the flicker, in turn, was a favored item in Perry's diet. The falcon, being chiefly a coastal bird, normally preferred to eat water birds but when Perry was inland he often preyed on this distinctive woodpecker.

The flicker had the woodpecker's undulating flight pattern and was brightly colored with golden brown striped wings and a flashing white rump that made him an easy target to focus on from above.

Perry was intently watching one now. The flicker was feeding on the ground, picking up ants with his long, sticky tongue. Perry wanted to take him on the wing. He waited.

Soon the unfortunate flicker decided to go elsewhere. He flew up over the open cornfield, an easy target. Perry launched himself downward directly from his perch. For this bird, smaller than a duck, the falcon did not use his foot as a club. Instead he swept down under the now frantically dodging flicker, turned on his back, and deftly seized the bird in midair with the mighty talons of one foot.

Scarcely slowing his speed, the falcon carried his victim back to the perch, broke its neck, leisurely plucked off the breast feathers, and had his meal. Then Perry flew off. The activity in the cornfield no longer concerned him.

Perry was wrong. The activity in this field, and in other fields in other places, was going to concern him greatly. As it was going to concern Pandion, the osprey now fishing near the mouth of an inlet that drained down from the field into the bay. As it was going to concern Baldy, the eagle scavenging farther down the bay. As it was going to concern, to a greater or lesser degree, almost all the creatures of the earth.

The farmer who owned the forthcoming corn lived in a comfortable two-story house just beyond the field, overlooking the long tidal inlet that extended up from the bay. He was a hardworking, middle-aged man who lived happily

with his wife and sixteen-year-old daughter. He was a good farmer and an educated one. He studied the latest agricultural bulletins, conferred often with the federal and state agricultural extension service people, and usually did what they told him.

In addition, he loved his fellowmen and most of the other creatures who inhabited the earth. This definitely, however, did not include aphids or anything else that might be a threat to his crops.

He was up early that morning, driving around his acres in an old battered jeep. He stopped every now and then to inspect his plants. What he saw were the aphids. If he saw the other insects feeding on this pest at all, he gave them no thought. Aphids were eating his tender young plants, and that was the only thing that concerned him.

He had been checking the corn every day, and now he saw that the situation had considerably worsened from the day before. He knew that a major infestation, one that might wipe out his crop, was threatened.

The farmer drove back to his house and telephoned a local crop-dusting service. The crop duster needed only the message. He knew what to do.

Early the next morning the crop duster readied his plane. From a large vat in the hangar he pumped into a tank on the belly of the plane a liquid consisting of water and a substance that is one of the "chlorinated hydrocarbons."

There are a good many of these chemicals, all relatives of DDT. They are a wholly synthetic chemical, alien to any natural process. Honors and awards were paid the men who concocted them.

With his tanks now full of this substance, the crop duster taxied out to his runway, took off and flew out to the cornfield. He dropped down to just a few feet above a corner of the field and pulled a lever in the cockpit.

Pumped out under pressure through thirty-nine nozzles on the undersides of the plane rained a mist, as the plane roared back and forth over the rows of growing corn. Half of the exuded spray settled on the corn plants and on the earth beneath them. The other half was wafted off in the atmosphere, some out horizontally to settle in other nearby places, some upward into the higher atmosphere to rain down days, weeks, or months later in faraway places.

The half that settled on the cornfield was devastating enough. Prey and predator alike were struck with sudden death. The small, soft bodies of the aphids convulsed as the poison attacked their nervous systems. Twitching in final spasms, they fell off the leaves and plants to die on the ground or they succumbed flattened out on the plants to remain there until rains washed them and their poison into the earth.

Adult predators, lacewing flies and ladybugs, sought to fly away as did the winged adult aphids. Overcome by the mist in the air they dropped back, convulsed and dying. The crawling larvae of the flies and ladybugs rolled themselves into tight, twitching balls as they fell to earth in their final convulsions. Ants leaped into the air a time or two before they also fell in spasms and finally lay inert.

The silence of death seemed to pervade the cornfield. But this silence was misleading, for not all were dead.

The birds, the most mobile of nature's creatures, had flown

off, frightened by the sound and sight of the low-flying plane or repulsed by the noxious spray. As soon as the mist cleared, however, most returned.

Now the birds had a bountiful feast. Instead of the effort and agility that had been required of them to catch healthy insects and larvae, their prey lay helplessly twitching and dying. Birds from neighboring fields were also attracted. There was plenty for all. Even some of them who were normally seed eaters, like cardinals and sparrows, could not resist helping themselves to the helpless and poisoned insect matter.

And in addition to the birds, there were other survivors in the field.

One of the many safeguards nature erects for her creatures is individual variation. Each individual of a species is at least a tiny bit different in physical attributes and in behavior from any other individual of the species.

Thus what may be fatal to one, another may be able to resist. It was almost as though nature had anticipated the devastation that was rained down on the aphids in the cornfield, and had taken measures to make sure that the species would survive.

Most of the aphids in the field were killed—but not all. There were at least a few with a little more resistance than the others. There were a few whose bodies were somehow able to produce a counteracting biochemical substance that weakened the poison.

There were a few whose outer skeleton was a little tougher, less penetratable than normal, and thus able to keep some of the poison away from the vital organs. And there were a few with a different behavioral response who were quick to get under leaves or other protective umbrellas.

Some of these aphids survived the slaughter. After a time they returned to the business of feeding and reproducing. Their offspring tended to inherit the characteristics that had enabled their parents to survive. New generations were soon being produced that were more resistant to the poison.

Some predatory insects and spiders survived, too, but not as many as the aphids. In the first place, there were fewer of them. In the second place, their more complex nervous systems seemed somehow less able to develop resistance to the chemical. And many that did survive went on eating the poisoned aphids until the toxicity did reach lethal proportions.

So, later that summer when the aphids were again feasting on the corn plants there were fewer predators to keep them in check. The farmer had to order additional spraying.

He harvested his crop. But that fall, when the eggs were laid again, they contained what next spring would be a new generation of aphids considerably more resistant to his poisons. He would have to reply with more or stronger dosages.

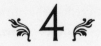

4

After watching the falcon fly away, Pandion had remained for some time resting on the top of the dead pine. Soon, however, hunger stirred in him and off he went, soaring slowly along the inlet eastward from the bay.

In the shallows he sighted a six-inch fish close to the surface. Folding his wings he came down headfirst, his talons thrusting forward at just the right moment. It was an easy catch.

But now Pandion was in for a surprise. As he came up from the water and shook himself, getting ready to take his prey to a perching place, the fish seemed suddenly to be growing bigger. It was, in fact, expanding rapidly and Pandion could feel his powerful talons being stretched out until they began to lose their grip.

The fish continued to grow until it worked itself completely free. Pandion's hoped-for meal plopped back into the water like a balloon. Almost instantly, the fish resumed its normal size and swam down out of sight.

It was a blowfish, or puffer. The peculiar defense nature had given it, the ability to inflate itself to many times its normal size, was designed primarily to help it avoid being swallowed by its usual enemies, larger fish. As an evolutionary by-product, as we have seen, it could also save itself from a hawk.

Pandion was going to waste a lot of energy on these peculiar fish. One time he picked up four of them in rapid succession and lost them all as they inflated themselves. From the sky they were very difficult to distinguish from ordinary fish that lacked the gift of self-expansion.

Frustrated now, Pandion went on hunting. Soon he was rewarded by sighting and capturing a normal fish. It was a good-sized one and Pandion came up from the water holding it securely with both feet. Before he started to transport it, however, as he had learned to do, he released one foot and secured a new grip well behind that of the other foot. Thus he was able to hold the victim lengthwise, parallel with his own body, and fly off with a minimum of wind resistance. He carried his catch that way to a tree limb where he could perch and leisurely feed after the manner of his kind.

Upon landing he released the rear foot, using that for perching, while he held his fish with the other foot. With his beak he plucked out the most conspicuous and easily removed parts, the eyes and surrounding flesh. Then, feeling along the fish's body with his beak until he found a place where he could bite into flesh, he pulled off quite a large chunk. This, with a backward toss of his head, he got into his throat and swallowed.

Before he was through, everything had been eaten except the toughest bones. Those he allowed to drop to the ground. In a short time, through his mouth, he would cast out a pellet consisting of the fins, small bones, and other indigestible matter.

His meal had taken close to half an hour. When he was finished, Pandion needed to clean himself. His beak, talons, and some of his feathers were soiled with the grease and oily substances of the fish.

Despite the fact that virtually all his prey was secured beneath the water so that, in effect, the osprey took a bath every time he caught a meal, Pandion liked to bathe for its own sake.

As a first step in the process, he left his perch and flew low over the surface of the inlet. He let his legs drop down and flew on dragging them through the water. When they were properly cleansed he rose, shook them, and pulled them up under his tail in the normal flying position.

He wanted now to clean his feathers, but for that he preferred fresh water rather than the salt of the tidal inlet. He climbed into the sky and flew inland to get a view of the surrounding countryside. He could see no freshwater pools or streams in the immediate vicinity.

So he returned to the saltwater inlet. It would have to do. It was too deep to stand in for a normal bath, so Pandion simply dived down in much the way he would if he were hunting. But this time his talons did not go forward. He hit the water headfirst and immersed his entire body. Flapping his wings and shaking his head, he plunged on through the water, dunking himself several times. When he had finished he rose, shook himself vigorously, and flew to a perch in a maple tree on the shore.

By now it was late afternoon. Pandion half opened his wings to let the falling sun complete the drying. Then he gave himself a thorough preening, running every feather he could reach through his bill, and he could reach almost all since the many vertebrae in his neck gave it a flexibility that mammals do not possess. The few feathers he could not reach with his bill, those on his head, he cleaned with his toes.

Finally fed, cleaned, and dried he bent his legs to lock his talons so he could perch effortlessly, and went to sleep.

He awoke just after dawn. He was hungry, a more or less constant condition, but he stretched and preened and waited. Although the thermals were not as useful to him as to those who hunted over land, they did help him gain altitude and were of some assistance in hunting close to shore. So he waited until the warming sun would produce these rising air currents.

In an hour he was in his usual hunting position, slowly flying and coasting some fifty feet above the shoreline, carefully watching for a silhouette beneath the surface.

Pandion was still a young and impressionable bird, endowed more than most species with that basis for learning, curiosity. While all his hereditary commands bade him catch fish, he had seen other birds catching other things. He had watched the falcon strike down birds and he had watched the eagle hunting other creatures in the water and on the land.

Anything that moved was apt to excite his curiosity if not his hunting instinct. So now, when he saw a strange creature hopping along the edge of a marsh, just off the inlet, he came down to investigate. It was a frog, so intent on pursuing its own prey, insects, that it had overlooked this threat from above.

When Pandion's talons closed on it, the frog's cry of

agony was cut short and ended in a gurgle. The osprey carried his victim to a limb and, tearing it in half, swallowed it in two pieces. When Pandion was a nestling his father had brought in frogs once or twice, so the taste was familiar, but he did not care for it nearly as much as he did for fish, and the meager amount of frog meat scarcely appeased his hunger.

He went on up the inlet, searching for a fish, but having no luck. He did see a dark object swimming just below the surface and curiosity got the better of him again. He dove and struck but his talons encountered no yielding flesh. He rose with his toes completely encircling the object but found he could not hold it. It was a turtle that had pulled his soft parts safely into his shell. Unharmed, he slipped out of the bird's grasp and dropped back into the water.

Pandion had had enough of experimenting. Now he flew on, searching more determinedly than ever for a fish. He was still, however, going to have one more lesson before the day ended.

A little farther up the inlet he saw quite a commotion in the water near the shore. Tiny minnows were leaping up from the water, some desperately throwing themselves clear onto the beach, where they lay panting and dying. Pandion was not interested in the minnows, but he was interested in a school of voracious bluefish that were driving the minnows onto the shore.

The blues were packed together and it seemed that he could not miss. He dove, and just as he did one of the fish made a quick turn seaward. It was a signal. In an instant the entire school turned away from the minnows and headed for safer, deeper water.

Pandion adjusted his dive and struck down among them. As his talons closed he felt only the tail of a rapidly swimming fish plunging free from him. He came up empty footed. He shook himself, and in frustration watched the school disappearing below his reach.

He had learned, and would remember, that seldom could he catch anything by simply diving into a school, no matter how tightly together the fish appeared to be. To be successful it was necessary to focus on a single target.

Hereafter, whenever he encountered a school of fish he would hover patiently overhead waiting for one to lag behind or get far enough from the pack to be a target. Singling out such a straggler away from the protective school, he would usually make a successful dive.

A little farther along, Pandion came to the farmer's house, the one Perry the falcon had seen the day before from the other side of the cornfield.

The white, two-story house was surrounded by tall shade trees, flowers, shrubs, and a lawn that extended down almost to the water where there was a dock and a small boat. Beyond the house and garden, Pandion could see the ocean of half-grown corn.

There was still some mist and noxious air above the field from that morning's spraying. The fumes might have driven Pandion away forever, but suddenly he caught sight of something he had been looking for for some time: a pond of fresh water. At least his experience told him that such ponds, separated from the inlets and the bay, contained water that was fresh.

This meant he could take a bath that would wash away the salt on his feathers. He dropped down and stood in six inches of clear, cool water. He ducked under the surface, wetting his head and body, and vigorously flapped his wings until he had doused himself thoroughly. Of all members of the big order of hawks, the osprey most enjoys a bath and takes one the most thoroughly.

Finally finished washing, Pandion flew up, shook himself in the air as he did after fishing, and looked for a perch on which to dry and preen. His favorite daytime roosts were the tops of dead trees, unencumbered by limbs and leaves.

There were no dead trees near the farmer's house and garden, but he saw a perch that would serve as well or even better: a utility pole that overlooked both the inlet and the pool in which he had bathed. Pandion landed on top of this and started his preening.

As he did so he took further note of his surroundings. There were many smaller birds in the garden and several different kinds were at a bird feeder full of seeds near the house. A family of cardinals, mother and father and two young on the wing, occupied it most of the time, but whenever they left, the smaller titmice, chickadees, and indigo buntings came to feed. There was also a suet feeder farther back from the house and this was being used, in turn, by a mockingbird and a downy woodpecker.

Pandion paid scant attention to these lesser members of his avian world. He looked down at the pond. There he saw a fish unlike any he had seen before. It was large enough to interest him, about six inches long, and it was bright red, a target he could not miss.

He left his perch, hovered over the pool, and dove. Just as he did so the door of the house opened and out came the farmer's daughter. She screamed and her mother and father came hurrying out. They watched Pandion rise and shake himself, the fish struggling in his talons. He carried his victim back to the top of the utility pole and began to eat.

The people were examining him closely. The farmer had run back into the house and returned with a pair of binoculars. They were passing the glasses back and forth studying the bird as he tore up the fish.

Pandion was just as curious about them as they were about him. He had never seen people as closely as this before. He would not allow them any closer—anything that moved, and was larger than he, was something to be wary of—but he felt no particular fright at these creatures.

He studied the three of them. They looked much alike to him, yet he could see that they were different from each other, just as each osprey he saw was different from any other.

He heard them making sounds and noticed that each had a different tone, just as each individual bird's sound was different to him. He knew the meanings of the sounds made by his fellow ospreys, of course, and could recognize individuals by their tone. And, just as their sounds and their appearances were different, Pandion was learning that there were other differences among members of the same species in the bird world.

Such differences were within strict limits, for nature would not allow the survival of an individual who varied too greatly from his fellows. But still, some ospreys were noticeably more sociable than others, some more aggressive, some quick to take offense at a real or fancied transgression, some willing to accept the intrusions of other birds.

These differences in behavior and disposition were readily communicated from bird to bird as they are from human to human. But at this point Pandion had no way of knowing that these same differences existed among humans and the sounds he was hearing from them meant nothing to him.

It is a pity, this inability of different species to communicate. If Pandion could have understood these people his life might have become much easier. Later, to a limited extent, he would learn to distinguish friendly from unfriendly humans, not by their sounds but by their actions. Now he could not know that this family was ready to welcome him.

Some people, who might have prized their goldfish, would have driven him off. Others might have tried to capture or even kill him. But this was a family who hated killing and did so only for survival. Had he been able to understand them, Pandion would have known he could settle down here without loss of freedom to a life of ease, protected from molesters and even given food if shortages developed.

As it was, when he had finished eating the goldfish, Pandion flew back toward the bay.

❧ 5 ❧

Meanwhile, farther down the bay Baldy, the eagle, was not having much luck with his hunting.

The fish he saw all seemed too lively and healthy for him to catch and the ospreys in the neighborhood were getting wary. They simply did not fish when he was around, thus depriving him of the opportunity of robbing them.

He flew along the highway in back of the bay looking for some freshly killed traffic victim. He dropped down where he saw a group of turkey vultures squabbling over the remains of a dog. He could easily have driven off the other birds and had the carcass to himself, but this dog had been dead for a good many hours.

Baldy would eat dead things, but not the old stinking dead that attracted the vultures. His carrion had to be at least fairly fresh. So he left the vultures to their feast and went searching over the meadows between the highway and the water.

Birds were not a common prey for him, since he could not very often catch them, but he always had his eye out for a bird in trouble. During the duck-hunting season he made it a practice to patrol the marshes and ponds where he would pick up quite a few wounded ducks, ones that after being hit could still get into cover and elude the hunter and his dogs.

The eagle, from a vantage point in the air above, could often spot one of these crippled birds and seize it before it could dive or get into cover too thick for him to penetrate.

But he had learned one lesson. The duck had to be able to move or Baldy would leave it alone. Once, in the dim light of an early morning, he had spied a small flock of ducks sitting in the water. He flew over them quite close. They failed to scatter, take flight, or dive or scurry for cover as they usually did if he got anywhere near them.

Puzzled, Baldy had circled back. When the flock still did not move it appeared that they were just unwary. He singled one out and swooped down as rapidly as possible, hoping to seize his prey before it ducked under the water or took to the air.

He was successful, but what a shock! Instead of the yielding flesh of a living bird his talons nearly broke on the hard, inflexible wood. He managed to let go and get back up into the air. As he did so the surprised eagle heard the laughter of men who were concealed in a nearby blind. He had tried to capture one of their decoys.

His feet ached for several days after that encounter and so, being highly capable of learning and remembering, Baldy never again attacked a sitting bird that remained motionless.

Now, a long time after that event, the eagle spotted a bird that seemed to be engaged in altogether too much motion.

It was a woodcock, a plump shorebird, and a relative of the sandpipers and snipes. Like ducks they were hunted, and Baldy had picked up crippled woodcocks in the past so he was familiar with them. But this bird was behaving very abnormally.

The eagle, like all wild creatures, was wary of anything abnormal. If what he saw did not release an instinctive response, or if it was something outside his experience and memory, he would hesitate—and this woodcock was behaving in a fashion far different from anything Baldy had ever seen before. Yet he was hungry, so he came down to investigate, landing on a tree limb a hundred feet away.

The woodcock was in a small clearing adjacent to some thick grass, where he ordinarily would have taken cover at the first sign of the silhouette of an eagle in the sky.

Woodcocks feed almost exclusively on earthworms, for which they probe deep into soft ground with their long straight bills, which are especially equipped with sensitive detection nerves. The hapless worm is simply sucked up and swallowed. Woodcocks have been known to consume their own weight in worms in a single day.

Since the bird thus spends much of its time with its head down toward the ground, nature has thoughtfully set the woodcock's eyes far back toward the top of his head so he can feed and at the same time keep a lookout for some enemy from above, such as Baldy. But now this woodcock was paying no attention to the bigger bird.

He had finished his nesting and had been getting ready to head south for the Louisiana marshes where he wintered. Before leaving he had to build up the store of fat in his body in case food was short on the long journey. He had recently feasted on an ample supply of worms he had found in the soft earth near human habitation. Nothing told him these worms were dangerous.

The woodcock had fed near a stately rural home. The couple who lived there had recently retired from the city and were proud of their country garden, especially the elegant maple trees surrounding it.

Two summers before, they had also admired some pretty little moths that appeared in the garden in unusual numbers, attracted by the lights in the evening. The admiration, however, had turned to concern when they learned something about these insects.

They were *geometrid moths*. Before dying off as the cold weather settled in, the females had deposited thousands of eggs on the trunks of the prized maples. In the spring these eggs had hatched. Out of them came caterpillars known as *cankerworms*, and before the elderly couple realized what was happening these voracious larvae were devouring the leaves of the trees. By midsummer there was fear the beautiful trees would be stripped bare.

The man and his wife called a tree-surgeon firm that sent out an expert to investigate. After examining the trees he recommended several applications of a DDT derivative. The chemical was applied and it worked. The trees were saved —but at a considerable cost.

Dead and dying cankerworms fell to the ground by the thousands, lethally poisoned. Birds and other predators ate many of them and carried away much of the poison in their own systems. Then the rains came to disperse this alien substance further.

Some of it was carried down into the topsoil. When heavier rains caused a runoff, much of it was carried into small streams, some settling in muddy or sandy bottoms, some washed along into estuaries of the Chesapeake Bay. Much of the poison still clung to the leaves of the trees and in the fall, when the leaves started falling, this was added to the toxic store already in the ground below.

While all this was going on, as the cold weather came and the soil hardened, the large population of earthworms in and around the garden had, after the manner of their kind, prepared for the winter. They had plugged the openings of their burrows with soil, and had dug down into the deepest part of their homes where more spacious chambers had already been prepared. Here, wrapped in tight little balls, either singly or in groups, the earthworms waited out the winter.

With the coming of spring and the softening of the earth, they began to emerge. And to feed. The earthworm is a filter feeder, like such mollusks as oysters and clams. But instead of filtering water through its system as these aquatic creatures do, the worm filters earth through its body, extracting as it does so the tiny seeds, microscopic larvae of various creatures, decayed plants and leaves, and other organic matter, alive or dead, that sustains its life.

But now something else was extracted from the earth before it passed out of the worm's body—poisoned earth. The passing season had not diminished the potency of the contamination.

The earthworm, with its relatively simple metabolic and physiological processes, was not much affected by the poi-

sons. But its body absorbed them, thereby building up large accumulations in its inner walls and digestive track.

The woodcock, like robins and other songbirds who were going to suffer similar fates, had been feasting on these worms for several days. The poisons, or at least a good part of them, were not excreted from the bird's body with the waste material. These insecticides do not dissolve in water, but they are soluble in fat. Thus they were absorbed into the fatty portions of the woodcock's body, constantly accumulating in large amounts.

After a few days the woodcock had become a little less active, but otherwise he seemed almost as impervious to the poisons in his body as were the lowly worms upon which he fed. However, he was not immune, for little by little the bird found himself less able to locate and capture his prey.

The day before Baldy appeared the woodcock had found few worms. To sustain him, his body had been forced to call upon the stored fat. The poison was thus released into the bloodstream and, as it was designed to do, attacked the nervous system.

When Baldy first saw the woodcock, the smaller bird was having a convulsion. He was lying on his back, thrashing about, moving his wings up and down in a hopeless attempt to regain his balance.

At one point the spasm appeared to be over. The bird managed to roll over on his belly and raise himself a little. But he stood for only a moment. Then he flopped down, his body twitching and head jerking. Suddenly he went into another convulsion. His body shook. He rolled over again on his back, his toes clutching at air, his wings beating helplessly.

Baldy, from his perch, watched this performance curiously. For the woodcock, dying was not easy. It went on for almost twenty minutes. Finally, however, in the midst of a violent spasm, his body relaxed and the bird lay quiet.

Baldy flew down and examined the dead bird. He could sense nothing wrong with it. Slowly, holding the carcass in one foot, he began with his beak to pull off some feathers and eat the still-warm, poisoned flesh.

The woodcock's troubles were ended. Baldy's were just beginning.

Soon the days began getting colder as well as shorter. Nature's main amphitheater of life started moving southward. Predator followed prey to warmer places.

Some raptorial birds would remain in northern areas for the winter, but the dwindling prey and intense competition for what remained would drive many to seek other places, especially the younger, less established birds.

As the northern earth cooled, so did its waters. Fish and other marine and aquatic life became less active. Fewer fish came to the shoals where they could be most easily caught by avian hunters. Pandion and Baldy and other fish eaters were beckoned southward. And as they and other birds left the area, so did those who preyed on birds, like Perry the falcon.

Thus, partly as just a simple matter of finding and following food, and partly as a response to the age-old migratory urge, active or latent in most birds, thousands of members of the great hawk family in the northern hemisphere started their fall flights southward.

Pandion, the young osprey, just wandered at first. He started working his way inland as the coastal regions were hit by early fall storms. He followed the rivers northward, but the cold and lack of food drove him to search toward the mountain lakes. Here it was colder and fish were even more scarce. Now, at last, he headed south.

It would be a long and tiring trip, but nature provided some transportation aids that would make it easier for those who knew how to take advantage of them. These aids would allow travelers to journey with a minimum of that precious energy that all creatures must husband for the more fundamental activities of securing food and eluding enemies.

Although it was Pandion's first long flight, he quickly learned how to take advantage of nature's aids for he had plenty of teachers. As he headed south he suddenly found himself in the midst of a great number and variety of his hawk relatives. These large birds were traveling along the great funnel of air currents known as the Hawk Mountain region of Pennsylvania. Pandion was quick to join them.

He had learned early to ride the spiraling upward thermals and occasionally he had felt himself buoyed upward by an "obstruction current," a wind bouncing upward off an obstruction like a hill or a building. Even flying over water, when he was low enough, Pandion could feel the upward lift of currents bouncing off waves, air currents often utilized by gulls, shearwaters, and other sea birds.

But never had he encountered anything like this. As the warm westerly winds struck the far slopes of this mountainous area, strong air currents swept upward. Pandion followed some of his more experienced relatives into a great updraft and was borne far aloft. From this height, Pandion found he could coast gradually downward, with just slight movements of his wings and tail to adjust his course. He could ride some eight or ten miles over the next rise until, near its bottom, another obstruction current would again bear him upward to repeat the process.

During these effortless rides, Pandion took note of his companions, other members of the great order of birds to which he belonged.

He was, of course, already acquainted with the peregrine falcon and here he saw some of the smaller members of that genus, the pigeon hawk and smallest of all, the ten-inch sparrow hawk. Like Perry, these smaller falcons also had the long, pointed wings and long tails adapted for pursuing their prey in the open.

Also among his many traveling companions, Pandion could see several of the *accipiters* or so-called "bird hawks" who, like the larger falcons, lived primarily on other birds. But these, the goshawk, Cooper's hawk, and the sharp-shinned hawk, all had short, rounded wings and long tails, for they often pursued their prey dodging through thickly wooded areas where the longer-winged falcons would have trouble.

Baldy the eagle was here, too, and a few of his western relatives—the all brownish-gold golden eagles. And there were also many hawks about Pandion's size that in silhouette resembled these eagles.

These were the *buteos* or soaring hawks, with chunky bodies and thick, rounded wings and short tails, birds adapted for soaring high over the earth and spotting prey on the ground below, mostly small mammals, snakes, and lizards.

Also traveling here were some large black birds, rather distant relatives of the hawks, but the most accomplished soarers and gliders of them all, the turkey vultures.

Together they rode the air currents bearing them to warmer regions and more plentiful prey, but the air currents could not last forever. Soon the mountains began to level off into the southern plains. The birds were above flat country and the free rides were ended.

Here they began to separate, each group and species seeking the habitat that suited them best. The buteos headed toward sparsely wooded areas, the red-tailed hawks sought out the dry areas, and the red-shouldered hawks went to search for marshy wetter places, while most of the broad-winged hawks kept heading farther south. Perry and the other falcons looked for open areas. Perry himself, preferring water to land birds as prey, stayed near the coastal areas as did Baldy, the eagle, while the accipiters headed for the thick woods.

For Pandion, almost exclusively a fish eater, water was a necessity. He flew on until he reached the headwaters of the Gulf of Mexico. Here food was plentiful, so he rested and hunted, and gradually worked his way farther south along the coast.

Finally reaching southern Florida, an area that was warm and where there seemed to be enough food, Pandion's travels for the time being were ended.

❧ 6 ❧

One day a few months later Pandion was perched at a favorite spot on the mainland edge of a broad sound in southwestern Florida. He was on top of a dead mangrove tree and had an unencumbered view in all directions.

Inland he could see marsh grasses and cattails surrounding shallow pools and seeping streams of mostly fresh water, an area seldom reached by the tides. Seaward, toward the saltwater sound where the mangroves began, the pools became larger lagoons and bayous.

In some places the water deepened, in others it remained shallow over extensive flats of mud and sand that were covered at high tide and exposed at the ebb. These were the tidal flats. Beyond them was the open sound, interspersed with a few small mangrove islands, and even farther out was a chain of larger islands between the sound and the open waters of the Gulf of Mexico.

The entire area was an estuary, the richest and most prolific of all places on earth. It was the cradle and nursery for large numbers and thousands of different kinds of life. It was here that the fresh waters of the land, rich in their terrestrial nutrients, eddied into the salt waters of the tides, even richer in the teeming life of the seas.

Pandion liked this area, and for a good reason. Here fish of the size he sought came into the shallows where they were easier for him to catch.

Some of these fish came to spawn, leaving their eggs clinging to plants or resting in the mud or sand. These eggs were hatching constantly, so baby minnows abounded and other larger fish came to feed on this fry, sometimes infanticidally on the very fish their own eggs or spawn had produced.

The smaller fish also fed on a vast variety and quantity of other life, much of it too small to be seen by human eyes. Here shellfish, oysters, clams, and snails of the great group of mollusks came to feed and reproduce, leaving tiny eggs and larvae. So did the Crustacea, the large blue crabs and stone crabs, the little fiddler crabs that darted in and out of their holes along the edges of the tides, and the hermit crabs that lived in the shells of dead mollusks, constantly exchanging smaller shells for larger as they grew.

There were insects. Mosquitoes laid their eggs in the drier areas, eggs that hatched when the waters rose. Out of these came the tiny mosquito larvae, the "wrigglers" that remained active as "tumblers" even when they reached the pupa stage of their metamorphic lives.

These offspring of the adult insects were a basic food for many species. Minnows of many different kinds fed voraciously on mosquito larvae and pupae and so did other things, including other insects, especially the ravenous larvae of the dragonflies, long wormlike aquatic caterpillars with a protruding underjaw that could be shot out half the length of their body to impale and haul in a wriggler or a tumbler. And while these young dragonflies were gobbling up mosquito larvae at the rate of twenty a minute, their parents were hovering up above, feasting on adult mosquitoes, some with as many as a hundred in their mouths at one time.

Almost all the great groups of animal life were represented in the estuary, from the invisible to the largest, the vertebrates. Of these, besides the fish, there were amphibians, reptiles, from tiny water snakes to large turtles and alligators, and mammals such as the otters and manatees that fed in the waters, and raccoons that patrolled the flats when they were uncovered.

But most predominant, in it, above it, and around it all were, besides Pandion, the variety of birds.

In the deeper waters the divers, cormorants, anhingas, grebes, and the diving ducks like scaups and mergansers, were, as was their nature, plunging down from the surface and pursuing their prey into the depths. The aerial divers were dropping from the sky as did Pandion, brown pelicans hitting the water with resounding splashes and scooping up fish with their netlike pouches, the delicate terns, dropping more gracefully and seizing tiny minnows with their bills, and the skimmers, with their knifelike lower mandibles cutting a furrow along the surface.

In the shallower waters the waders, herons, storks, and ibis were feeding off little fish, shrimp, baby crabs, eggs, and larvae of insects. Farther inland, along the edges of the water, the great variety of shorebirds were feeding, plovers seizing organic matter found on the surface and sandpipers with their longer, slimmer bills constantly probing into the mud or sand.

In the air Pandion could see still more birds, the noisy gulls scavenging or seeking to rob some other bird, and the martins, other swallows, and the nighthawks pursuing microscopic insects in flight. Such was the incredible richness of life along the shore, where the land meets the sea and fresh water mingles with salt.

Of all this teeming life of mud and sand and water most was the friend of man, seen or unseen. Only one creature, and that only in the form of an adult female, was the declared enemy of man, the mosquito. And now, for her sins, almost all were going to die.

From his high perch, Pandion was among the first to see and hear the huge, noisy, and ugly object approaching in the air. It was an airplane, flying low over the marsh. Suddenly from its undersides came streams of noxious vapor, poison mixed with oil.

Pandion left his perch. The other birds below left their places in the water or along the shores. They could escape, at least temporarily, the noise and the eye-smarting vapor. Most of the other residents of the area, not endowed with wings, would have to take it.

The plane flew back and forth until the entire region was blanketed with a thick, brownish mist. Some of this would settle into the water, vegetation, and soil below, some would wash out with the tides into the sound and seas beyond, some would travel with the air and winds and settle into distant lands.

The pilot finally exhausted his tanks and flew back to his mosquito-control headquarters to report the successful first "sublethal application." There were some deaths in the estuarine area from this application, but many of the aquatic animals were able to avoid direct contact with this first poison that had come raining down onto their world.

The free-moving forms sought escape in the deeper water. Rooted shellfish, like oysters and clams, simply clamped their twin shells shut and stopped feeding. The univalves, or snails, pulled in their opercula, closing up shop.

Thus biological activity stopped. But it could not stay stopped for long. The fundamental processes of eating and being eaten must go on. After the plane had left and the mist had dissolved somewhat, the inhabitants of the estuary began to return. The vital activities of life were resumed—but with a difference.

The poison permeated the water and clung to the microscopic animal-vegetable plankton on which fed the tiny free-swimming larvae of mollusks, Crustacea, and insects. It began to accumulate in their bodies.

They, in turn, were now again being eaten by the minnows and other small predators that were also the prey of larger fish and birds. In the fatty tissue of each body the poison was dissolved and stored, accumulating in higher concentrations in each step upward along the food chain.

Two weeks later the plane returned and the estuarine area received another, similar treatment. This time there were more immediate casualties, and when the life processes were again resumed there were signs of erratic behavior.

Some of the poison of the first application had been dispersed by the tides and currents, but much of it had remained in the plants, the mud, the sand—and in the bodies of the inhabitants. And it had lost none of its potency, neither that which had drifted away to infect other places, nor that which remained. The second dosage was simply added to the first.

This lethal chemical was designed to attack the nervous systems of its victims, and it now began to take effect. Pandion, on patrol over the waters, sighted a five-inch fish. He hovered, waiting to anticipate the depth and direction with which this hoped-for meal would try to escape.

Down he came and to his dismay struck the water a little ahead of his prey. The alarmed fish rather sluggishly escaped into deeper water. Pandion had never seen a fish move so slowly. He had allowed too much on his dive.

For now there was a noticeable decrease in agility, a lack of speed and sureness, in both predator and prey. Pandion soon learned to adjust his strike in mid dive if he saw his victim moving more slowly than normal. Soon he was catching more fish more easily than he ever had before.

Other predators—birds, larger fish, and other animal eaters—unless they themselves had become too sluggish, were enjoying a similar bounty. The poisoned prey was rapidly being eaten and assimilated. The healthy, agile victim was passed up in favor of the unhealthy, easier-to-seize one.

Soon the plane returned for a third application. The disaster now was nearly complete. Pandion, coming back after this spraying, beheld a scene of devastation.

Many minnows were on the surface of the water, swimming erratically, zigging and zagging. Others were twitching and trembling, half over on their sides. A few had thrown themselves clear out of the water onto the shore.

Along the shore hundreds of fiddler crabs were trying to get back into their burrows where they would die in privacy. Few could make it. Some of the little crustaceans were stumbling, scarcely able to crawl. Others were lying flat, writhing helplessly. The big fiddlelike claws of the old males were twitching without purpose.

In the water the target for all this, the mosquito larvae, were dying. So were those who fed upon them. Besides the little fish, the dragonfly larvae, and other animal eaters, prey and predator alike were experiencing spasms and convulsions.

There were many that came now to prey on the dead and dying. Big blue crabs and snails began attacking the helpless minnows and insect larvae that were dying faster than they could be eaten.

Soon most of the minnows had stopped twitching and were lying still, floating bellies up in the water. The shore was littered with the bodies of other minnows and of the small fiddler crabs. The larger blue crabs and other aquatic predators continued to feast on the dead.

Pandion watched all this without leaving his perch. Overhead he saw Perry, the falcon who had come flying over to see what was going on. Neither Pandion nor the falcon, nor, as a matter of fact, the terns and skimmers and the diving cormorants, anhingas and ducks, would take dead prey unless driven to it by extreme hunger. But there were other birds that would.

The first to return to join in the feast were the noisy, squabbling laughing gulls who started gobbling up the dead and crippled minnows. They were soon joined by vultures and fish crows. And then appeared a larger, more majestic bird with white head and tail. This was Baldy. The other birds moved aside to give him room. The eagle often ate carrion so he, too, joined in the feasting.

There were now swarms of larger fish in the shallows. They had come, like the crabs and birds, to feed on the moribund minnows. Many of the larger fish were already sluggish from previous feedings on poisoned prey and some of them, adding to this earlier toxicity, were also in the throes of death.

They were swimming erratically, coming to the surface gasping. Some started twitching and some turned over and floated upside down despite desperate attempts to right themselves. But, however abnormal their behavior, many of these larger fish were still alive.

Pandion was watching them. He was hungry and it was not in his nature to pass up anything as easy as this. He left his perch and went into a dive almost immediately. His target was an eight-inch weakfish, or sea trout. Despite an adjustment, a checking of speed in mid flight, Pandion almost overshot this prey.

The fish made no attempt to escape. He stayed on the surface, swimming about in little circles. Pandion seized the weakfish easily, carried him back to the perch, and started eating. He did not notice an opaque white film covering the eyes of the still weakly struggling fish. It was blind.

Even as he ate, Pandion kept watching his old enemy, the eagle, ready to fly up in case the robber once again should attempt to steal his meal.

But Baldy had no reason to bother the osprey. Instead, he left the shoreline where he had been feeding on the minnows, flew out over the water, and himself picked up a larger fish. Even the more clumsy eagle could easily catch this half-comatose prey. It was easier than accosting the osprey. Baldy would stuff himself while he could.

Perry the falcon, up above, was also hungry. Fish were not to his liking nor was he equipped to catch them if they had been, so he waited. Soon one of the laughing gulls, stuffed with poisoned minnows, decided to leave.

She had flown only a little way up into the air when the birds below heard her agonized screams of alarm. She turned sharply, desperately trying to reach the comparative safety of the cover offered by nearby mangrove trees. Perhaps, had her stomach been less full, she might have made it. As it was she did not have a chance.

Perry, at tremendous speed, hit her with a clenched talon. The gull was knocked fifteen feet forward and downward and Perry easily seized her with one foot before she reached the ground. He carried her to a higher, drier area and holding her with one foot started plucking and eating. These overfed birds were easy prey so Perry, too, would stuff himself while he could.

Meanwhile, the other birds went on with their feeding. A hungry, hunting falcon would have had them scurrying for cover. A feeding falcon was usually no immediate threat.

Soon there began another wave of death in the estuary. The larger blue crabs and stone crabs began to react as the smaller fiddlers had earlier. They ran about erratically, twitching. Convulsed and in spasms they fell, unable to rise. The poison, attacking their nervous systems, was producing erratic behavior, pain, convulsions, and finally, death.

The chemical had been developed to kill insects and they were its most immediate victims. But crabs, shrimps, lobsters, and crawfish, although they appear to be quite different, are, in the broad scheme of things, rather closely related to the insects. Along with the predatory spiders they are all advanced arthropods, segmented and jointed animals, with very similar physical, nervous, and bodily structures.

What was fatal to insects was ultimately fatal to them, too. These Crustacea, having gorged themselves on poisoned death, were now paying the price.

Some days later there would be other deaths in the marsh. Some frogs went into convulsions and died. So did a few small snakes. These amphibians and reptiles were terrestrial vertebrates, like birds and mammals, including man. With them it was just taking the poison a little longer.

⁊ 7 ⁊

Few things are more cleansing than the tides. After a few
ebbs and flows the estuary seemed to be back to normal. The
dead were eaten, the sick soon succumbed to predators, and
the remnants of bones and skeletons were washed away. The
survivors resumed their normal activities.

Unlike the Crustacea, which had suffered wholesale killing, and unlike their own free-swimming larvae, approxi-
mately 90 percent of which had been killed, the adult
mollusks seemed little affected.

Oysters opened their valves and resumed pumping some
eight gallons of water through their systems each hour, out
of which they extracted enough nutrient to survive. But now
they were also extracting something else. Concentrations of
the poison in their succulent bodies would be found to be
some seventy thousand times what it was in surrounding waters.

The carnivorous snails, the univalves, from tiny marginellas
to giant conchs, continued to feed on hermit crabs that had
died in their borrowed shells and sunk to the bottom, and on
any other remains of the recent victims they could find.

There were other survivors, of all kinds, for no species was
completely wiped out. It takes some doing to eliminate a

form of life that nature has, through thousands of generations, equipped to survive. It can be, and has been done but usually with more advanced, specialized creatures. And unless a species is wiped out completely it will usually breed back to a stable population, or outsiders will move in to occupy whatever habitable environment is left for it.

Thus baby crabs soon reappeared, looking like tiny insects with transparent bodies and huge eyes. Baby shrimp came swimming or floating in from the open waters where they had been spawned.

There were survivors among the insects, too. Especially among the "target" insect, the mosquito. Wrigglers reappeared and soon developed into tumblers. And after them came the larger insect larvae and the minnows, and after them the larger fish and the birds.

The estuary seemed to return to normal, but this was misleading. A potent new factor had been added. Poison remained in the sand and mud, on the vegetation, in the nontidal waters. But most of all, in incredibly higher concentrations, it remained in the bodies of the inhabitants.

Pandion, like the other predators, had made the most of the bounty of feeble prey. However, when the living and the half-dead were gone, and only corpses remained, hunting for him was not so good. Eaters of dead flesh would remain. Before the apparent return to normal and the reappearance of sizable fish to the shallows, Pandion had set out to explore elsewhere.

He flew off across the sound on one foraging expedition and searched along the inland shore of one of the larger islands that lay between the sound and the open gulf. Here there were wide expanses of water only a foot or two in depth during normal tides. The water was clear, the visibility good.

So here, on the other side of the sound, Pandion established a perch on the top of another dead mangrove tree. He liked to be able to see in all directions and so preferred a vantage point with no small limbs or leaves above him. He did not use a perch as a hunting outlook from which to launch an attack, as Baldy and Perry and other predatory birds often did, and so did not need the concealment offered by a living tree.

Pandion's hunting was all done as he soared slowly, or hovered, over a shore or open water. And he was now as adept at it as he ever would be. He had learned to adjust his altitude to the visibility and depth of the water below, hunting from thirty to a hundred feet in the air.

He seldom plunged down into the water unless he was reasonably sure of securing prey, but even so it was not much more than half the time that he would emerge with a meal.

He had learned, the hard way, that a four-pound fish was about the heaviest he could handle. Once he swooped down, attracted by a larger fish. The strike was true and the victim was seized. But instead of Pandion rising with the fish, the fish went down with Pandion.

For a terrified moment he struggled to disengage his talons as he was pulled completely under the water. Just in time he worked himself free and rose to the surface. He never again struck so large a fish.

Pandion also discovered that, after catching a fish, the sooner he got it ashore or onto a feeding roost, the more apt he was to enjoy it. He had had the experience of robbery by the bald eagle up north, and several times since coming to Florida he had been forced to relinquish prey to this marauder And he had learned, in this semitropical area, that there were other pirates of the sky that were even more formidable.

His first experience with these came one morning when he was flying ashore with a seven-inch jack struggling in his talons. He saw a shadow on the water and, looking up, perceived above him a large black bird with a long forked tail and long, very narrow wings, even longer than the wings of the eagle.

It was a male frigate bird, or man-o-war bird, a quite properly named buccaneer. Pandion attempted to increase his speed and sought to get above what he instinctively knew was going to be a tormenter, but with the fish in his grasp he was unable to do so.

The frigate bird was quite close to him now and Pandion saw that he was facing more than one attacker. Approaching were two more of the pirates, a female with a white breast and an immature bird with a white head.

The nearest assailant, the all-black old male, came alongside and threatened to strike the osprey with his powerful, hooked bill. Experience told Pandion that the game was up. He released the fish and the frigate bird swept down and neatly seized the loot in his bill.

But this was not the end of it. The other frigate birds, perhaps disgruntled because they could not share in the spoils, began to vent their displeasure on Pandion. One on each side, they forced the osprey to turn and head back over the water.

They persisted in this maneuver, frustrating every attempt by the smaller bird to gain the safety of the shore and the trees.

Frigate birds are powerful creatures in the air, able to fly tirelessly for hours. Pandion was soon exhausted. He feared being forced down in the water where his assailants might peck him to death.

Finally, however, with a sudden downward swoop he was able to get by the attackers and land on the shore. He half ran and half flew under a tree and the frigate birds flew off. Hereafter, whenever there was more than one frigate bird in the sky, Pandion went to hunt elsewhere.

Now and then Pandion saw the noisy, monstrous creature belching its noxious fumes that had driven him away from his hunting grounds on the other side of the sound.

He stayed away from it, the prospect of dead fish not being attractive to him. But there was no complete escape from the output of this plane, or from many others in many parts of the world, any more than there was escape from the poisons and other pollutants draining down from farms and factories, homes and boats along the waters surrounding the estuary.

On his hunting trips, anywhere in the sound, Pandion often saw fish swimming erratically near the surface. They were easy prey, and whenever he spotted one of these sluggish fish of the proper size, he would swoop down and seize it. Nature, ever anxious to preserve the energy of her creatures, commanded that whatever could be taken with the least expenditure of energy should be seized.

Other birds were obeying the same commands. Many of

the fish with near lethal toxicity in their systems were minnows, too small to interest Pandion. But this fry was being gobbled up by other birds—herons and egrets, terns and pelicans, cormorants and other divers.

Pandion was also seeing a good deal of Baldy lately, although the eagle seldom paid much attention to him. While Pandion avoided the areas visited by the spraying planes, Baldy was attracted to them.

As a matter of fact, Baldy's daily routine diet was undergoing rather drastic change. Seldom did he find it necessary to rob Pandion, a rather arduous method of securing a meal, since, unless it seemed hopeless, the osprey usually resisted and made it as difficult as possible.

Baldy had also almost entirely given up his early morning patrols of the highways in search of mammalian and avian traffic victims. And seldom did he pursue coots and other birds that he had occasionally managed to catch in the past.

There was an easier living now. Baldy, and others of his kind, had discovered the increasing numbers of fish which they, with their limited fishing abilities, could capture. And they had quickly learned to associate the appearance of a low-flying, belching plane, with the presence of this bountiful prey.

Thus when such a plane had concluded its mission, and as soon as the foul-smelling mist had lifted sufficiently, Baldy would head for the area. He knew he would find there a plentiful, if tainted, feast.

He had competitors. If the spraying took place on a windless afternoon and the mist was not dissipated sufficiently until near the end of the day, Baldy would usually lose out.

He could not see well enough in the dark to hunt or scavenge.

Often he would return to a sprayed area at dawn only to find most of the dead or dying fish gone. Raccoons and other nocturnal mammals also regularly patrolled areas where the visit of a belching plane could be expected to have left some easy prey, as did many birds after sick minnows, night herons, roseate spoonbills, and other nocturnal or crepuscular feeders.

Even in the daytime, Baldy would often have to drive away competitors. Once, landing on the shore of the sound after the poisoned mist had risen, he found that he had been preceded by a group of vultures.

A black vulture, the more aggressive of the two species in the area, was trying to tear up a dead fish while three of the more timid turkey vultures were standing by anticipating that some of the feast might be left for them.

Baldy's arrival, however, forced everyone back one step on the ladder of precedence. At the sight of the eagle, the black vulture moved aside docilely and took his place among the waiting turkey vultures.

Baldy seized the fish and with his strong talons easily tore it in half. It was a mackerel that had been feeding voraciously for several days on minnows which, in turn, had been gorging themselves on mosquito larvae that had been subjected to unusually concentrated spraying.

The mackerel, a usually robust fish, had been sick for two days but had managed to elude his enemies and continue to eat more of the minnows until he finally died.

Baldy now gulped down a beakful of the dead fish. It

seemed to him to be unspoiled, freshly killed, and fit for him to eat. But even to the bird's poorly developed sense of taste, it somehow seemed odd. The eagle took another bite and his hunger left him. He flew off with just a part of the mackerel in his stomach.

The black vulture, his hunger stimulated by watching the other bird eat, now returned to his prey. Lest something else come to interfere, he hastily bolted down all of the remains soft enough for a vulture to eat, as he lacked talons and a strong beak to tear into his victim. Nothing but disappointment was left for the turkey vultures who flew off to resume their ceaseless, gliding patrols.

The black vulture, however, also sensed that something was wrong with what he had just eaten. He promptly regurgitated, ridding himself of the meal. Vultures regurgitate easily, which would prove to be an advantage that would permit them to outlive the eagle.

It was now spring in the semitropical southland and the population shifts this would bring about were beginning. There were departures for the north and arrivals from the south.

Many of the arrivals would not stay long. Some shorebirds, many warblers, and other songbirds who had wintered even farther south would linger only a few days or a week before pressing on to nesting grounds in the north.

Others, such as black-necked stilts, least tern, cuckoos, vireos, and gray kingbirds up from the south after an absence all winter would stay and nest. Some of these birds would go on and nest farther north.

One arrival who would nest only in this area now was a

member of Pandion's big hawk group, the swallow-tailed kite. Pandion watched one of these graceful birds, with its white head and underparts, black back and wings, and long forked tail.

It was deftly seizing grasshoppers and locusts in the air as they flew up from the grassy fields. Once it even swooped down to pick up a small water snake from the surface, and accomplished this without getting even its legs wet. It consumed all this prey as it continued to soar.

Of the departures most of the ducks, with their full breeding plumage and many of the pairs already formed, would head north first. They would be followed by all the gulls except the small laughing gull, and most of the shorebirds, some of whom, including the tiniest sandpipers, would journey into the arctic circle, forming their pairs en route.

There were many species of which some members would migrate while others remained. Pandion was one of these. Some of his fellow ospreys were departing for the north while others, permanent residents, would stay and nest in the southland.

Pandion himself was a northern bird and there stirred within him the call to return to the area where he had started life. He was now a year old and outwardly, at least, was a fully developed bird. He had not undergone a molt since acquiring his first plumage. That would come later. But his coloring had changed nevertheless.

The buff tips on the feathers of his first-year plumage had now worn off. The darkish hue that made him a recognizably younger bird had thus given way to a lighter color, giving him all the whiteness of an adult.

But despite this appearance, Pandion was still a young bird. The migratory urge might be felt but it was weak. Later, when it would be coupled with a breeding urge, Pandion would be bound to return to his home area to seek a mate.

Now, as most one-year-olds and some two-year-olds of his kind would do, he would remain mateless throughout the forthcoming summer on these wintering grounds.

This was not true, however, of Baldy the eagle or Perry the falcon. They were both older birds. Many of Baldy's fellows were permanent residents and would nest as well as winter in the south. But Baldy himself was a northern bird. As he had in years past he was heading north with the spring. He could expect his mate to join him at their nesting site.

As for Perry, his kind had never nested in the flatlands so far south on the eastern coast of the new world. The falcon had left quite early for northern areas where there were cliffs on which a proper aerie could be established.

8

From his perching place on a ledge near the top of a twelve-story building, Perry the falcon could watch the life of the city below him.

It had been almost a year since he had left Florida and events had conspired to lead him into this domain of the creatures he once had so feared. It had taken time, but he had finally overcome, at least partially, his feeling of the special enmity of man that had resulted from the kidnapping of his youngsters.

So now, like a throwback to some ancient ancestor who had inhabited the turrets of medieval castles in feudal Europe, the falcon had come two months before to make a temporary home in these artificial heights.

There was a great deal of activity below him, to most of which he paid little attention. There were the large bipedal creatures walking about or riding in various vehicles that belched noxious fumes into the air. Some of the walkers would stop now and then to peer up at him, but most paid no more attention to him than he did to them.

There were often other mammals in sight. Dogs and cats and, especially in the early mornings and evenings he could see rats. These rodents never seemed to lack for food: trash thrown in gutters or left in parks, or unattended garbage containers. There always seemed to be enough litter left about for the rats to sustain themselves. And Perry saw only the rats that ventured out-of-doors in their foraging. He did not know there were many more of these little mammals finding enough to live on inside the buildings and houses that made up the city. For, like most of men's cities it contained more rats than people.

But it was not mammals, big or little, that kept the falcon in what would seem an alien environment. It was his normal prey, the birds, that had led him and quite a few others of his kind before him, to leave the ledges of their cliffs and take up temporary, or even long-term residences on the ledges of the artificial cliffs men constructed as their habitats.

When Perry had left Florida in the early spring, nature strongly bade him to return to his own nesting cliff overlooking the Chesapeake Bay and its inlets. If all went as nature planned, his mate also would return there.

Both birds would be attracted more by the urge to return and claim their territory than by the urge to rejoin each other. But the results would be the same. After the necessary ceremonial preliminaries, nesting and raising of young would take place with both parents participating.

As far as Perry was concerned, he behaved as scheduled. He arrived at the nesting cliff first, as the male usually does. He then simply stayed in the area awaiting his mate. She failed to arrive.

This, of course, is not unusual and is something well provided for by nature. If his old mate failed to show up she was probably dead and she could be dead from a wide variety of causes. Perry would wait only so long. Then he would try to interest the first wandering female that came along, either a new bird or one that had lost her mate.

However the falcon was already becoming a rare bird, especially in the eastern United States. No female falcon appeared. After a time Perry himself took to wandering. There could be a female that had lost a mate and yet had stayed on the territory awaiting the possible arrival of another male.

But Perry could find no such prospective mate and by early summer his springtime desires had left him. With no family cares or ties he embarked on a nomadic existence until one day he sighted in the distance a darkish and mildly fetid mass of air. His curiosity led him to investigate. Under this blanket he found himself in one of man's cities.

He probably would have left it at once, but the fetidness was not quite at the eye-smarting stage and the bird, with his poorly developed sense of smell, could tolerate the odor.

He was attracted by a high building overlooking a river. A cliff over a river or over some body of water was his normal dwelling place, so this seemed ideal. In this environment he always found the prey he liked best—water birds of one kind or another, flying along or over the rivers. And here the prey would be out in the open where he could best make an attack.

But now he was going to experience a new kind of waterway. He sat on the ledge over the river for a long time and saw no life whatever except for men and rats. He saw trash and other debris in the river, but no birds. And no sign of fish or other animal life or any aquatic vegetation that might have served to attract the birds on which he hoped to prey.

He had better look elsewhere. As he flew up to leave the dead and dirty, lifeless river, he caught sight of a bit of greenery surrounded by more man-made cliffs. It was a little city park and in it he saw birds.

He was hungry so he landed on the twelfth-story perch overlooking the park to take stock. He saw none of the water birds that he preferred, but there were meals enough here if he could catch them.

There were, as a matter of fact, just three kinds of birds, species that seemed to find life best in the proximity of man and all of which man himself had brought into the new world: house sparrows, starlings, and pigeons.

The sparrows were too small to interest Perry very much. He would most like a pigeon. It was a bird just about the right size for him and he eyed those in the park carefully. They were all very close to people, some of them gobbling down food almost out of the hands of people sitting on benches.

While Perry had overcome some of his fear of men he would never, of his own free will, get that close to them. So reluctantly, and despite his hunger for these unusually plump-looking birds, the falcon took his eyes off the pigeons and looked elsewhere.

On the grass, some distance from the walks and benches where the people were, Perry saw a dozen starlings diligently searching for the insects, insect larvae, and edible vegetable matter on which they thrive.

As the falcon watched, the starlings suddenly flew up. Perry launched his attack, trying to single out one individual as a target. The starlings, however, maintained themselves in a tight, compact flock and before the falcon could stoop at an individual they all disappeared into the branches of a tree at the edge of the park.

As a matter of fact, Perry eventually would kill quite a few starlings, for the birds were not always that wary, or that lucky. But they were a difficult prey and usually managed to get into the cover of trees, onto the ledge of a building, or simply close enough to people to frustrate an attack.

As it turned out, he was going to have the same kind of trouble obtaining a pigeon. He returned to his perch, his hunger increasing. He concentrated now on the pigeons. Sooner or later they would have to fly and would get far enough away from the people to be vulnerable.

It was getting late in the afternoon and shadows were deepening. Perry was content to wait. Hawks are diurnal hunters but Perry could see better than most in the half-light of dawn or dusk. He had often caught birds going to or coming from night roosts.

So it would be now with the pigeons. As the darkness began to set in, those in the park rose in flight. They were not in a compact flock as the starlings had been, and Perry had no difficulty singling out one pigeon that lagged a little behind the others.

He had to wait, however, until they were some distance away from or above the people. The pigeons headed for the ledge of another building where they customarily roosted.

They were in no great hurry. Except for cats and an occasional boy with a BB gun, they had few enemies in the city and they felt their lives to be secure.

The feeling of security tends to relax normal cautions and is a luxury few wild things can afford. The pigeons circled up high on an apparently carefree flight before going to roost. Perry climbed into the sky above them and began his stoop.

At that moment the pigeons sensed this unaccustomed danger. With increased speed they headed straight for a building even taller than the one on which Perry had been perched. Perry adjusted his dive. His only hope for a meal now was the one laggard who was desperately trying to catch up to the rest of the flock.

The pigeon could not quite make it. Just before he reached the comparative safety of a window ledge, Perry seized him. The falcon was unable to turn or stop in time, so he bumped into the window and almost lost his prey. Shaken, he carried the feebly struggling pigeon back to the perch where he ate it and went to sleep.

Perry was awake the next morning before the pigeons, but when they left their roosting ledge they flew closely together straight down to the park. Hereafter they would be more cautious and thus make things even more difficult for this newly arrived enemy.

Once again Perry was about to leave the city and seek easier prey elsewhere. Suddenly, however, he caught sight of a single pigeon, flying a steady course over the river that had been so unproductive the day before.

Here was just what he wanted. A single bird, easy to focus on and unwary enough to be flying too far from cover to be able to elude him.

Perry left his perch, climbed slightly above the bird, and launched his downward stoop. The pigeon is a fast-flying bird and this one was especially so. He was traveling at more than ninety miles an hour.

With rapid wing beats as he came down at an angle now, the falcon was flying at least twice as fast. The gap between the two closed. At the last moment, the pigeon tried to shift its course but Perry turned also and as he passed over his victim he seized it with one talon without even slackening his speed. The pigeon, which a moment before had been flying desperately, was now hanging limply in the falcon's talons.

Perry carried the pigeon back to the perch for plucking and eating. The people in the waking city had been unaware of this little drama in the skies above them. Only a few even knew Perry existed, but now things were going to be different.

The evening before had been dark and rather windy when he had come back to the ledge with his first pigeon. The feathers from his plucking had been dispersed and had not been noticed. Now, however, it was a bright, windless morning. The feathers from his latest victim came drifting down from the ledge, visible to all.

From that time on he would often see groups of people looking up at him from the street.

It would be nice to report that under these circumstances his behavior would be such as to meet the approval of those

[86]

watching him. But this was not to be. For judged by human standards, Perry would be branded a wanton murderer.

During the next few days Perry continued to make his headquarters on the ledge overlooking the park. He caught a few unwary starlings, but the pigeons stayed close to the people and seldom flew. When they did, it was only to go directly and together to or from their roost.

Then, one morning, he again saw a lone pigeon flying a rapid, steady course over the river. Perry caught him with ease. When he was halfway finished with the pigeon, he saw another bird flying in the open far from cover.

There is a streak of what man would call ruthlessness in the falcon. Even when hunger does not move him, the sight of a bird just asking to be seized can bring on an attack.

Perry dropped his half-eaten prey and set out in pursuit of the second pigeon. He carried this one back to the ledge but almost at once he saw a third one flying over the river. Again he attacked and again, while he was carrying his victim back to the ledge, another pigeon appeared.

Perry dropped the bird he was carrying and made another kill. Altogether that morning he killed six pigeons and ate only part of one.

Through the centuries the favorite food of peregrine falcons, at least for those away from seacoasts and near the haunts of men, has been pigeons—especially racing and homing pigeons that tend to fly in the open and on a straight course.

This liking has brought about conflicts between men and falcons and between men and men; so the consequences of Perry's actions would not be unique.

Pigeon racing has long had a popular following, especially in Europe where, until quite recently, rewards for dead falcons were offered in some places by organizations of pigeon fanciers. Certainly many of Perry's ancestors had died or lost their eggs or young at the hands of enraged pigeon owners. The killing of falcons to save pigeons has also taken other forms. In addition to racing pigeons, for thousands of years men have used them to carry messages. And despite modern developments and the use of more sophisticated methods of communication, as late as World War II both sides used homing pigeons for this purpose.

During the war the British Royal Air Force hit on the idea of using falcons to disrupt this enemy communication. Peregrines were trained to intercept pigeons used by the German army.

But the British discovered that at home, presumably without any urging by the enemy, peregrines were destroying their own pigeons that came bringing in messages. Between 1940 and 1945 some six hundred young and adult falcons were destroyed on orders of the British Air Ministry.

So, the men in the city where Perry had taken up residence who now wanted him killed, or captured and taken away, had precedent to back them up. But Perry had defenders too. Bird lovers banded together and demanded that he be protected and encouraged to remain. They pointed out he was an extremely rare bird and that he killed starlings as well as pigeons.

While the bird remained passively unaware of it, this conflict between men raged below him, both sides finally demanding that the city councilmen decide the falcon's fate.

Fortunately for them, in the end it was Perry himself who settled the matter.

During most of Perry's stay in the city, the days had been quite windy after a morning calm. Now, however, came a spell of calm weather.

The pollutants in the air became thicker, and while he still might tolerate the odor, Perry's eyes began to smart and his lungs and respiratory system became irritated.

One day he simply flew away, leaving the city to its pigeons, starlings, house sparrows, and people—including the greatly relieved members of the city council.

9

Pandion the osprey was now two years old. He had spent most of his life quite contentedly in the southern wintering grounds. Now, however, vague longings and discontents were beginning to stir within him.

For many of his kind these stirrings would not occur, or at least would not be strong enough to compel action, until the young fish hawk was three years old. A few, however, do go forth to seek a territory and a mate in their second year. Perhaps Pandion was endowed with this precocity of emerging into full adulthood ahead of time. Or perhaps it was a reaction to the tainted substances he was storing up in his body, nature somehow sensing that he had so little time to live.

At any rate, the complicated and mysterious chemistry of spring was at work, apparently stimulated by the catalyst of warm and lengthening days. It was giving commands that Pandion had to obey.

He started north. At first he traveled in easy stages, stopping for a few days wherever he found good fishing. Then as spring advanced he felt an ever-increasing urgency to return to the area where he had started life.

He worked his way up the coast and after some days came to the mouth of the Chesapeake Bay. Without a stop he flew over the congested waterfront areas there. Then he slowed down, for he was hungry. He soared and hovered, hunting over a series of broad estuaries that in the past had supported so many of his ancestors: the mouths of the James, the York, and the Rappahanock rivers.

The only signs of life he saw were human. As far as Pandion was concerned these estuaries were dead. Finally, after flying some eighty miles along the bay shore, just before reaching the Potomoc estuary, he sighted fish some distance out in the bay. The water was a little deeper than that in which Pandion preferred to hunt, but he did catch a half-pound perch. He carried it to a tree where he consumed it and settled down for the night.

The next day he continued working his way along the western shore of the bay until he came to the narrow section where his life had begun. Although he had not been in the area for two years, and then only for the first few months of his life, the surroundings were all etched in his memory.

He passed over the inlets where he had first learned to hunt, but the nest in which he had grown up was nowhere to be seen. The tall trees that had lined the shore were all gone. In their place Pandion saw a complex of buildings, metal towers, and wires. Men and bulldozers were below, transforming the once lush shoreline into a nuclear power plant.

Pandion flew on. He remembered following the falcon along this route. He came to the spot where Perry had gone inland but once again the osprey stayed over water, following the long inlet that led to the farmer's house by the cornfield where he had fed and bathed.

He found the fishing better here and had fed himself before

he arrived once more in sight of the farmer's house. Pandion had less fear of humans than most birds of prey. He might be repelled at man's work but not at man himself, provided, of course, that what he regarded as a safe distance was maintained between this large earthbound creature and himself.

What Pandion wanted at the moment was his own territory. It did not have to be a large area, such as was demanded, for example, by Perry the falcon or by Baldy the eagle. They usually would not tolerate another of their kind within several square miles of their nest.

Pandion could be satisfied with just a few feet as long as one essential requirement, that there be a site for a nest, was fulfilled. Pandion was not particular about the type of site available either, except that he did not like to have any branches or other obstructions above the nest that could interfere with his vision or his approach.

What he liked most was a tall dead, or half-dead tree on the very top of which a nest could be built, rather than having to build it down in a crotch. Such sites, however, were often unavailable so he had to be prepared to settle for much less. He had seen osprey nests on the top of muskrat mounds, almost on the ground, or on low man-made buoys only a few feet above the water.

He had also seen them on the tops of poles. And this is what attracted him now. He had once perched on one of a line of utility poles leading to the farmer's house, and on the very top of one now, a few hundred feet from the house, he saw a small platform, some two feet in diameter.

Pandion landed on this platform and looked around. His

view in all directions was unimpeded. He could keep a long stretch of the inlet and surrounding territory under scrutiny. He was far enough from man's habitation so as not to feel uneasy about that, and he was close enough to the freshwater pool to use it for bathing. The spot seemed ideal.

There were just two other essentials—food and a mate. There were still fish in the inlet and along the shore of the bay, so the requirement for food was fulfilled. The other was not going to be so easy.

Pandion now made his headquarters on this platform near the farmer's house. He did not venture far from it. Another male might come along and usurp the site, or an available female might wander by that he would miss.

He returned to the platform after each hunt to eat his prey and he roosted there at night. He saw just a few other ospreys in the area and they were always in pairs. They paid no attention to him unless he ventured too close, in which case an aggressive gesture was all that was needed for him to keep his distance.

On the second day a lone osprey appeared in the distance. Pandion left the platform and climbed skyward, crying as he did so: *Cree! Cree! Cree!* But the bird flew on. It was another male.

The next day another, slightly larger osprey appeared. Again Pandion climbed into the sky with the territorial and mating cries. This time the newcomer landed in a tree across the inlet and watched.

Pandion was excited now. He climbed a full thousand feet into the air, turned, and with half-folded wings shot downward, continually calling *Cree! Cree! Cree!* He leveled off, turned a somersault, climbed again, and repeated the maneuver.

The strange bird left the tree, swooped down to the ground to pick up a foot-long stick, and brought it to the platform. Pandion swooped down until he was a hundred feet over the inlet. He glided slowly until he caught sight of a fish. With extra deftness he dropped down and rose from the water with the victim squirming in his talons.

Shaking the wetness from his feathers, he carried the prize up above the platform and hovered. The newcomer crouched and begged: *Pseek . . . pseek . . . pseek!* She was advertising her femaleness. Pandion landed, tore off the head of the fish, and gave the rest to the other bird. He had his mate.

The two started fishing and roosting together. The bond was sealed and strengthened and mating soon took place on the platform.

Pandion's consort was older than he. Since she was the mate of royalty, we will call her Nassa, which would have meant "Queen" or "Lady" to those who named Pandion.

She had been mated to another osprey several miles down the bay and the year before they had raised two youngsters. They had separated, as they had in past years, until spring had drawn them both back to the nesting territory.

Nassa had gone south along the ocean shore, fishing in waters still kept fairly clean by waves and tides. Her mate had gone inland, fishing along rivers and lakes surrounded by men's farms and factories.

With spring he returned to the nesting site but his behavior was aberrant. He evinced no interest in Nassa. She crouched and begged in the accepted manner. He drove her off. Finally, he was the one who left. She had last seen him flying an erratic, zigzag course toward the south.

She had waited a few days but when no replacement appeared she, too, had left the territory. She had been drained of the desires of spring, but the encounter with Pandion and the sight of his courtship performance had served to renew her urges.

Now she and Pandion lost no time. They both started searching for fallen branches and sticks that they carried to the platform. At first they carried in the largest pieces they could find and handle. Pandion brought in one dead branch that was four feet long and two and a half inches in diameter.

Nassa soon stopped collecting material herself. Instead she began locking the pieces together to form the nest. Pandion began gathering smaller pieces; when he had trouble finding them on the ground, he broke live twigs off a willow tree and laid them before his mate. After this he brought leaves and grass to the platform. Nassa took this material and formed the softer lining of the nest, and at last it was ready.

Or almost ready. There are certain adornments that seem to be necessities in an osprey's nest. While Nassa was putting on the finishing touches, smoothing out the lining and packing it down with her body, Pandion went searching for whatever decorations might meet his fancy.

He first brought home a large cork float that had broken loose from a fisherman's net. Next Pandion arrived with a child's shoe, and later with a piece of blue oilcloth. All these objects were carefully placed in the completed nest.

Nassa, meanwhile, was occupied with other duties. In a few days she made her own contribution to the contents of the nest: an egg two and a half inches long and two inches thick, its basic pinkish-white coloring almost completely covered with splotches of deep reddish brown. She started incubating at once, although two more eggs were to follow to make up the normal complement of three.

Until this time, Nassa and Pandion had fished together, sometimes sharing their catches, if only one were successful, sometimes each eating his own. Now, for the next thirty days, the providing would fall on Pandion alone. Only rarely would Nassa leave her nest and eggs. She would be dependent on her mate for food, and sometimes she would be very demanding.

Her irritability was perhaps augmented by the fact that during this month of enforced nonactivity, nature had arranged for Nassa to change all her feathers. While she was incubating she would experience her complete annual molt.

Pandion, on the other hand, would not start changing his feathers until he had completed all the redoubled activity required by the cares of fatherhood. Not until the young were grown and able to take care of themselves would the male osprey start his much more prolonged molting period.

But whether the cause was her molt, her lack of exercise, or something else, during this time Nassa would often express her displeasure.

At times Pandion would fly around a bit with a fish in his talons before coming to the platform, and once or twice he landed within sight of Nassa and tore off the head for himself before bringing her the rest. At such delays her outraged begging cries could be heard clear into the farmer's house.

The farmer and his family, delighted that their platform had attracted the birds, were keeping them under careful observation and, if the truth be known, were helping Pandion a bit.

Fish were not nearly so plentiful in the Chesapeake Bay area as they were only a few years before when the region supported many more ospreys, even some fairly large colonies of the social fish hawks. Pandion often had trouble finding suitable prey and, when the hungry youngsters came along, it was going to be even more difficult.

He might not have been able to manage at all had it not been for the fact that the farmer had a friend who was a commercial fisherman. Every few days his boat would pull up at the farmer's dock with a pail containing several medium-sized fish. These would be freed in the pool, into which salt water had been pumped so they would live. This deprived Pandion of his freshwater baths, but he was more than compensated by the easy prey.

After the young were hatched, Pandion continued to bring in most of the food for the brooding mother as well as for the youngsters. At first Nassa would tear off tiny pieces of the fish for the babies, feeding the youngest first and making sure all three got fed.

When they were a few days old, the babies were able to keep themselves upright and soon learned to tear off pieces of fish for themselves. As they grew, their appetites increased, and Pandion was severely taxed with constant trips for food.

More and more he came to depend on the stocked pool near the farmer's house.

The farmer and his family tried to keep a distance away from the pool most of the time, but unless they were right next to it their presence did not bother Pandion unduly as soon as he got used to them.

He learned to recognize the three of them, the rather tall, gaunt man, the older woman, and the daughter. Pandion often made dives into the pool after fish when one of them was in the yard. Occasionally, when one of them wandered close to the nesting pole both he and Nassa would watch but would make no remonstrance.

When a strange person appeared, however, both ospreys would become alarmed. When the farmer's family had company in the yard, Pandion would not approach the pool, and if a stranger came near the nesting pole, both he and Nassa would scream their protests.

Their real fright came, however, when a crisis developed in the farmer's household. It was a power failure. The electric cooperative sent out a repair crew that determined that the trouble lay on the very pole on which the cooperative had previously granted the farmer permission to build the platform in the hope of the osprey's return.

A linesman informed the farmer that that pole would have to be climbed, but he promised to disturb the birds as little as possible.

And so, as Pandion and Nassa watched with growing alarm, a stranger stopped below their pole, buckled on his climbers, and began his ascent.

Both old birds flew up from the nest and started circling about, screaming their protests: *Kareee! Kareee!*

As the man got closer to the nest, Pandion dived down at him, missing him by only a few feet. The linesman continued his climb until he reached the wires just below the nest.

Now Nassa changed her cries. *Kew . . kew . . kew!* The week-old youngsters understood. They froze, lying flat on the bottom of the nest, absolutely immobile.

The linesman quickly completed his repairs and then, unable to resist satisfying his curiosity, raised himself another few feet and peered into the nest. What he saw he would never forget.

Young ospreys do not have whitish down like most other baby hawks. They were covered instead with lacy strands of cinnamon and pinkish brown, which blended perfectly with the dead grass, leaves, and twigs that lined the nest and on which they were lying.

From the skies above a predator might well believe the nest to be empty. Even the man, peering over the edge, at first thought the babies were dead.

But then he saw one thing that had been overlooked. Although the babies were lying flat and limp, playing dead to perfection, their huge yellow eyes were wide open and, even at that tender age, glared defiance at this intruding stranger.

❧ 10 ☙

The linesman who went up the pole and disturbed the ospreys had made one mistake, and because of it the youngsters in the nest were now in mortal danger.

The climb had been made in the middle of a sunny day, a time when the mother was always careful to stand over the babies to shield their tender, featherless bodies from the heat of the sun.

By the time the linesman had descended and the old birds dared return, the youngsters had absorbed a great deal of heat and lost a great deal of moisture. They were panting rapidly, their bodies' desperate attempts at internal cooling.

The sight of her young in these straits released some age-old reaction in Nassa. She swooped down to the inlet, dipped her breast feathers in the water and, still dripping, returned to the nest. Now she stood, bending over the babies, allowing the moisture to drip onto their burning bodies while with her wings outspread she sheltered them from further ravages by the sun.

It worked for the two elder youngsters, for they finally cooled off and their pantings slackened. But the smallest, the one hatched from the last egg laid, was too hot and dessicated to be saved. His pantings continued but they became feebler and feebler as his young life ebbed away.

As the remaining babies grew larger—and hungrier— they still would accept what was given to them with a minimum of squabbling and allow each nest mate to eat in peace. The mother osprey, however, was much more forceful in expressing her demands.

When Pandion approached the nest with a fish in his talons, he was given to announcing his arrival with a soft, chirping food call. This was not necessary. Nassa could discern his approach when he was on the horizon. She immediately would go into her begging crouch and make her desires known by a series of sharp whistles.

As he had done when he had to provide food only for her, when she was incubating the eggs, Pandion sometimes came in with a whole fish and sometimes with a decapitated one, for if he were hungry enough he would still eat the head himself before returning.

And he would still very often make a circle or two over the nest before finally landing. This had annoyed Nassa when she had only food for herself to worry about. Now that there were youngsters to be fed as well, her irritability was heightened.

Sometimes she seemed about to leave her nestlings and pursue her tantalizing mate, but she never did. Instead she increased her cries and as soon as Pandion came within reach she would grab at the fish with her beak or a talon. Often there would be a brief tug-of-war before Pandion released his prey into her possession.

Nassa's eagerness for the food, it always turned out, was her compulsion as a mother rather than her own hunger. Once having secured the fish from Pandion, she immediately started tearing off the pieces to give to the babies. She ate little herself and did so only after seeing that all her charges were fed.

Of course there would occasionally be squabbles, especially as the babies grew a little older, stronger, and more obstreperous. But for the most part the entire process was remarkably amicable. The young refrained from attacking each other or from attacking their parent as do so many other hungry nestlings.

And so, when the smallest brother died from exposure to the midday heat, his little body lay in the nest untouched. In the nests of most other carnivorous birds he would have been eaten.

One evening Nassa finally, as a matter of nest sanitation, picked up her baby's body and dropped it over the side. During the night the ospreys were awakened by the growls of two raccoons fighting over the morsel, and by daylight there was no sign of the little body, so the farmer and his family were spared the knowledge that the restoration of their power had cost a life.

While Nassa had rid the nest of her baby's body, which otherwise would have spoiled and become a health hazard, she was not so tidy with the remains of the fish she and the youngsters ate.

There was no danger of a health hazard here. Everything but the bigger bones and fins were eaten. Nothing that could spoil was left. If these white bones were just dropped over the side, an enemy on the ground might be aided in locating the nest. For many things—snakes, raccoons, skunks, and other mammals including men—do climb up and rob osprey nests. It is just as well the nests are not advertised any more than necessary.

The parent ospreys had not acquired the habit of carrying these remains away from the nest and dropping them as many birds do. Instead they simply let them accumulate. The fish bones and fins could make things uncomfortable for the young, so Pandion, in between food trips, would sometimes bring in small sticks, twigs, or grass that Nassa would weave into the bottom of the nest, thus both concealing the remains and keeping the resting place softer for the young.

The old ospreys paid little attention to other birds, unless they were known marauders who might try to steal an egg or seize a baby. Such notorious thieves as crows and jays were driven off if they ventured too close.

Smaller birds often nested undisturbed in the lower branches of osprey nests. Here, near the farmer's home, a pair of house sparrows was raising young in a nest built in the underparts of the osprey nest.

Not only did they have a fine, protected place for their home, the sparrows were also defended from the marauders that were driven off by Pandion or Nassa.

As the young ospreys grew, they started climbing around the nest and flapping their stumps of wings for exercise. Their appetites increased correspondingly.

Pandion now spent almost all his time fishing just for them, eating little himself. By instinct and training he was accustomed to hunt over a wide area. Even though easy prey was often available in the farmer's pond, he still spent much time searching over miles of shoreline along the inlet and the bay.

Sometimes his hunting carried him down the bay and across the narrows, to the shore where he had started life. He avoided the immediate area. Men, bulldozers, and buildings did not attract him, and, anyway, experience had taught him that the fish he sought were seldom found where these things were about.

A good deal of the shore on both sides of the bay remained much as he had left it two years before, with one great difference. Then he had often flown by the nests of fellow ospreys, some within a few hundred yards of each other. Now he could go miles without seeing a bird although sometimes he sighted the remains of nests, neglected and deserted.

In the past there had also been several pairs of those big marauders who had tried to rob him, the eagles. Now it was not until one day some time later, when he was fishing along the western shore up the bay from where he had originally encountered him, that he was confronted again by Baldy.

The big white-headed white-tailed bird and his mate had occupied their same nest again this year and, late as it was in the spring, were still incubating eggs.

It was midafternoon when the confrontation took place. The eagle had been hunting for several hours without success. Back at the nest, he had set on the eggs during the morning while his mate went out to hunt and feed herself. For the eagles, like many members of the hawk order, took turns incubating their eggs. Baldy and his mate spelled each other on the nest, unlike Pandion and Nassa whose domestic arrangement called for her to do all the incubating while he brought in the food.

Now Baldy felt it was time to return and relieve his mate. But he had not yet obtained any food for himself. This time when he relieved her she would not be back until dark, and Baldy would spend a hungry night if he did not manage to find food before he returned.

He had followed a time-tested routine. He had patrolled several miles of highways where he often found carcasses left by men's vehicles, but this time without luck. Leaving the roads he had soared over some marshland until he sighted a flock of coots in open water.

There was a tree nearby in which he could conceal himself. He waited until he saw one of the birds apart from the rest and quite a distance from any protective reeds. He tried to come down quietly, but somehow he could not control the fluttering of a wing, which gave him away.

One of the coots sounded an alarm. Those near the reeds skittered across the top of the water to safety. Others dived and swam under the water.

Baldy's target, a young female, went down and swam desperately under the surface in the direction of the reeds. Baldy anticipated this and tried to adjust a return dive to the time and place where his hoped-for prey would have to emerge for air.

The coot, a vegetable-eating bird the size of a small duck, is a slow flyer and, with semiwebbed instead of fully webbed feet, a rather clumsy swimmer and diver. In the past when Baldy was able to get into a hiding place and attack one of these birds by itself and a hundred yards away from cover as this one was, he could usually manage to catch it.

But now his timing seemed to be off. The coot came up for

air before Baldy started his second dive. She was able to draw two full breaths before he forced her to dive a second time. No matter. Usually, if Baldy could force one of these birds to dive and swim for its life under the water, it would finally grow so tired that he could pick it up.

The eagle rose and made a third dive, talons outstretched hopefully. This time the coot had progressed farther than he had anticipated and came up out of his reach. After the fourth dive, Baldy found it was he who was growing tired while the coot seemed as alert and evasive as ever. Reluctantly the eagle gave up and flew off seeking other prey.

It was then that he sighted Pandion.

He had not found many ospreys to rob recently, but his familiarity with the proper tactics had not been lost. He kept well behind Pandion and, as long as he was able, kept a row of trees along the shore between him and his victim.

Pandion, for his part, was concentrating on his fishing. He had seen so few eagles this spring that he had lost some of the wariness that had often enabled him to detect this enemy and abandon a hunting grounds if one appeared.

Now his hungry family had been without food for several hours. He was headed back toward the nest but he would not return empty footed. Soon he caught sight of a disturbance along the shore ahead. Some fair-sized blue fish were pursuing minnows into the shallows.

Pandion singled out one silhouette, folded his wings, and dived. As he came up and shook the water out of his feathers, shifting his grip on the struggling fish, Baldy appeared far above him.

The eagle screamed and dived. Reluctantly, Pandion was about to release his newly caught prey. Experience had long since taught him that, alone and encumbered with a fish, resistance would only be a waste of energy.

But now something told him that this would-be robber was not so formidable after all. On his present dive the eagle was going to miss him by twenty feet. Instead of releasing his prey, Pandion started to climb into the air himself. If he could avoid the eagle and get above him, he had a good chance of carrying his fish home.

Baldy came down, talons outstretched. When he saw that he was wide of the mark he hastily struggled to change his course, but Pandion was already above him and climbing rapidly. The eagle began to pursue him but, still tired from his fruitless encounter with the coot, he soon gave up.

Baldy returned to his own nest and a hungry night. His body would have to draw on its fat. He would be even less able to face his problems the next day.

As a matter of fact, in addition to a sluggishness and at times a lack of coordination that could not be attributed to age—he was only seven and many of his kind lived five times that long—Baldy had other troubles.

After losing their young the year Pandion was hatched, Baldy and his mate, sometimes together, sometimes apart, had both drifted south. Unlike the young osprey, they had returned the next spring. They had performed their courtship rites—for even though they were mated for life these yearly formalities were carefully observed—and had built up the old nest they had been using for the past several years.

Two large white eggs had been produced and the birds started taking turns incubating them. They had been feeding well and continued to do so all spring, finding that many fish that previously had been too elusive for them to catch were now rather sluggish and so were easy prey.

The eagles incubated the eggs for the normal five weeks. There was no sign of hatching. For another six weeks the pair went on, carefully turning the eggs at intervals and keeping them warm twenty-four hours a day.

Finally, after more than twice the normal incubation period, the urge that bade them to tend the eggs subsided. They flew away and left the now rotted eggs to some disappointed crows, they being by then inedible even to these omnivorous creatures.

Still, the commands of nature had not left Baldy and his mate. This second spring they returned to try again. This time they did not feed as well. There were far fewer fish, whether hale and elusive or poisoned and sluggish.

Otherwise everything was the same. When he encountered Pandion, Baldy and his mate had been incubating for ten weeks. For the second year they had sterile eggs.

❧ 11 ❧

As Pandion continued up the bay, carrying back to his family the fish he had saved from the eagle, he was unaware that still other eyes were on him.

Perry, the falcon, was watching Pandion's somewhat labored flight. The osprey was tired from his encounter with Baldy and was still encumbered by the fish in his talons. He would be easy sport for the falcon. As we have seen, almost any bird, flying a straight course out in the open, could usually tempt Perry into a few practice dives, if not an actual kill.

But Perry felt a listlessness now that was hard to overcome. Only when hunger drove him would he leave this ledge high on the cliff where he was perched. And then he was all business, out to make a quick kill for food.

There was no more of the playing that had once been an outlet for his zest for life. No more ventures high into the atmosphere, followed by dives and loops, all for their own sake, all of which he used to find so exhilarating. Now he usually felt too weak and often too tired.

After the noxious air had driven him from the city, Perry had wandered inland for a time. Here he had lived mainly on land birds that fed around farms and pastures. But with the beginning of the spring warmth the old urges had drawn him back to his nuptial territory, to the cliff over the bay where he had nested in the past.

He was again in search of a mate. This time he would find one.

Perry first saw her when he was perched on the limb of a tree at the back of the cliff. While she was still just a speck on the horizon he started his cries:

Wichew! Wichew! Wichew!

Stimulated, some of his old vigor returned. He launched into an aerial performance, climbing upward until he almost disappeared, then diving downward at tremendous speed.

As some birds display colorful plumage or intricate songs, Perry, after the manner of his kind, was displaying his most distinctive attribute: his magnificent power of flight.

His first great diving loop was followed by more aerial acrobatics, food offerings, and continued cries, and soon the pair bond was formed.

All did not go smoothly. It soon developed that there were some differences in the desires and behavior of Perry and his new mate. Perry had become used to spending much of his time away from the seacoasts, accustomed to a diet of land birds, especially seed eaters like the pigeons in the city. This prey was by no means free of contamination, but Perry, while often tired and listless, still had most of his sureness on the hunt. His stoops were still swift, his accuracy unerring.

This was not altogether true of his mate, who had been living on a more deadly diet. She was younger than he, only three years old. Perry was her first mate. Like many of the peregrines native to the middle Atlantic region she was only weakly migratory, differing from the northern peregrines, most of whom regularly traveled each year between the frozen lands and the tropics and beyond.

So Perry's consort had spent most of her days in the Chesapeake Bay area, moving only a little south in the colder weather as she followed the prey she liked.

She had been living primarily on water birds and, especially as a young bird with much still to learn about the arts of securing prey, she was attracted most often to those that were easiest to catch.

By and large these were the fish eaters, the diving ducks, grebes, and terns. These birds she often found less wary, more apt to be where she could attack, and less skillful in trying to avoid her stoops. Thus, as they fed mainly on sluggish fish, she fed mainly on the sluggish birds.

Perry, of course, was unaware of any of this as he and his newly won mate, as was customary, began to hunt together. This was a ritual that would further cement their pair bond prior to the egg laying and the onset of parental responsibilities.

On the first morning out, their different appetites brought them to cross-purposes. Perry wanted to go inland to some open meadows and valleys after the land birds that were now his more accustomed prey. His mate, however, attempted to coax him after her toward the water.

The birds circled each other until Perry, calling in persuasion: *nye-ah . . . nye-ah . . . nye-ah!* set forth resolutely inland. His mate followed. For this first hunt, at least, Perry had proved to be the dominant one.

The two falcons soon sighted a flock of about twenty red-winged blackbirds in the air far ahead of them. They climbed upward and increased their speed.

Without any previous learning, each knew his assignment in this cooperative venture. The first objective was to break up the flock. When he was only slightly behind the blackbirds, Perry came down in a comparatively slow dive. His mate continued her flight well above him.

Perry screamed as he approached the flock. Although the terrified blackbirds scattered in confusion, Perry made no attempt to capture one. His mission was accomplished. His mate could now center on a single bird, and since they were in the open it should be an easy target.

Down she came after the outermost blackbird. Perhaps because she was more accustomed to pursuing sea birds that flew differently, perhaps like some of her prey she was herself sluggish and uncoordinated, whatever the reason, she missed.

The frantic blackbird saw her speed by beside him. He pumped his aching wings even harder in an attempt to reach the shelter of some trees. But Perry had also seen his mate miss her target. With a couple of strokes of his long wings he overtook and seized the luckless blackbird.

Perry carried this prize to his mate who was now perched on a limb, resting. She accepted it and started plucking as Perry went off after his own meal.

Thereafter they did not try to hunt inland again. Instead Perry followed his mate along the shore or over the water. Here she did a little better. These were birds with which she was familiar, fish-eating sea birds, and often they were unnaturally slow in their reactions. Still, even here, she missed more often than she should and on a good many occasions Perry picked off a duck or other prey that had escaped her.

So far, for the two falcons, the mutual hunting and their companionship was all preliminary. They had not yet started their nesting.

As was usually the case with peregrines it was the male who first had the strongest urge to raise a family. When the pair returned from their hunts, Perry would land on the ledge in the cliff.

Nye-ah . . . nye-ah . . . nye-ah! he would cry as he sought to persuade his mate to join him. She, however, seemed reluctant. She would circle about above him or land on a tree limb while Perry explored different parts of the ledge.

Like all American falcons, but unlike most other hawks, Perry and his mate would not build a nest. In several different places on the ledge, which was some six feet long and twenty inches wide all under a slight overhang, Perry scratched away at the dirt and debris.

He was making the beginning of shallow hollows, or "scrapes," where eggs might be deposited without rolling over the edge. His mate was still not quite ready, so after this unsuccessful coaxing, Perry would fly up and join her and they would roost and sleep on a tree limb.

The female falcon, in fact, was delaying things much longer than normal. If all had been well she would have responded very quickly to Perry's invitations to nesting. Finally, however, just before Perry's own urges might have worn off, his mate was overtaken with her delayed desires.

Now she took command. She landed on the ledge and, ignoring the several slight depressions Perry had fashioned, she picked a spot of her own, as far back from the edge of the ledge as possible, and started scratching at the dirt with beak and talons.

When she had a hollow some two inches deep, she rounded it out with her body. Perry went off to hunt. Because Perry was now going to have to capture enough food for both of them, he continued to hunt over the water and shoreline, seeking the easiest victims. Whenever he sighted a bird flying more slowly than normal, or with slower reactions, he would make a quick kill.

The first egg was laid the day after the female had come to the ledge; the second was laid two days later. She then started incubating, although a third egg would follow in another two days.

In the normal course, the female would incubate the eggs alone for about the first two weeks, after which the male would begin to spell her at times to allow her to get in some exercise by hunting for herself.

Unfortunately, the normal course was not going to prevail.

While his mate was incubating, Perry brought her food to her. When he approached the cliff with a limp bird dangling from his talons, she would leave the eggs long enough to come out and meet him. Perry would then transfer his prey from foot to beak and, as she flew under him, he would drop it for her to catch. She would then carry the prey back to the scrape where, resuming her job of keeping the eggs warm, she would pluck and eat.

At first this worked normally enough. But on the third day, although she was only a few feet directly below him, she completely missed a large royal tern he dropped for her to catch.

Perry swooped below and retrieved the bird before it reached the ground. He then brought it directly to his mate, who had returned to the ledge. Thereafter, when he came in with food, she did not fly out to meet him. Instead she remained on the ledge, crouching and begging: *Waa-ahk . . . waa-ahk!* Perry would toss the food onto the ledge for her.

During this time Perry kept himself well fed and well cleaned but he did not neglect the paternal duties nature bade him fulfill.

After he had brought food to his mate, he would usually go off to search for his own meal, although if he secured an especially large bird he might eat some of it himself before bringing it to the nesting ledge.

He often bathed, but he was careful to do so only in the shallowest water by the shore. And he got himself only partially wet. Unlike Pandion, or even Baldy, the falcon would never immerse himself or take a chance that he might have to. A prey bird that managed to get out to deep-enough water would usually escape.

After eating and bathing, Perry would usually perch at the top of the cliff or on the ledge near his mate. Here he would carefully preen his feathers. During all of his activities, hunting, bathing, preening, he was constantly on the lookout for intruders.

He considered at least a mile along the bay shore as his territory, and trespassers beware. Especially to be kept away would be a direct competitor for the food he needed for himself, his mate, and his hoped-for family. That, of course, would be another peregrine.

But, although in previous years Perry had often defended the cliff against many such intruders, now he saw no other falcons at all. He and his mate seemed to be the last of their kind on the Chesapeake Bay.

He did not pay much attention to most other birds that might wander by, unless he was hunting, but he was constantly on guard against intruders who might offer a threat to his eggs or his young. Once he saw Baldy as the eagle made a slow, lumbering flight up the bay, but the big bird did not venture close enough to warrant an attack.

Sometimes Perry could combine territorial defense and hunting, securing food, and doing away with an enemy at the same time. Once a fish crow, a constant scavenger for the eggs and young of other birds, had wandered too close to the cliff. He provided a meal for Perry and his mate.

The mate, meanwhile, was beginning to behave strangely. Often she would ignore the food Perry brought her. And when she saw him approaching, instead of making the soft begging calls she would sometimes warn him away with a loud protest: *Cak! Cak! Cak!*

Then one morning, when she was turning her eggs, as she had to do quite often, one of them broke. She had rolled it over with not much more than the usual force of her bill and had it been a normal egg nothing would have happened.

But it was not a normal egg. Her body had failed to produce sufficient calcium, or failed to have it available for the formation of the egg as it came from her body. The shell was paper thin. As it rolled over it cracked and the contents started to seep out. She looked at it in bewilderment. She pecked at the crack with her beak, opening it wider. Slowly she began to eat the contents.

When she had finished eating the broken egg, she methodically cracked open the other two and ate their contents also. There were no signs of beginning embryos. The eggs had been sterile.

Perry arrived back at the ledge with a sandpiper in his talons to find his mate standing amid the broken shells. Then he heard her cries.

Cak! Cak! Cak! She lunged at him. Puzzled, but under no instinctive urge in this case to fight back, Perry flew off the ledge. Still clutching the little shore bird in his talons, he circled about.

His mate, however, now came after him in earnest. Perry dropped the sandpiper but she ignored it and it fell to the beach at the foot of the cliff. With further defiant cries his mate flew at him. Perry fled.

At this point she seemed to lose interest in him altogether. He perched on the limb of a tree and watched. His mate circled about, climbing higher and higher into the sky. She made a series of loops and climbed still higher.

When she was only a speck in the sky she folded her wings and went into a downward plunge at tremendous speed. Perry could hear the wind whistling through her feathers.

Finally she started to level off but when she did so she was headed straight for the face of the cliff. She failed to swerve. Her speed, mercifully, granted her an instant death. She crashed into the cliff and fell to the bottom with a broken neck.

❧ 12 ❧

While Perry's mate had become demented and Baldy and his mate were trying to hatch eggs without life in them, Pandion and Nassa were better off. Unlike the falcon or the eagles, the ospreys were raising young.

Nassa's molting was complete now and often Pandion would stand guard over the nest while she went off, brandishing her new feathers, to hunt for herself. She would not bring in food—that was Pandion's job. When she returned, exercised and fed, she would relieve Pandion at the nest so he could go out and fish for the youngsters.

The babies were now large and active enough to get their downy heads over the edge of the nest and stare down at the world around them. Sometimes, with their great yellow eyes, they would gaze curiously down at the farmer who was often seated out in his yard. And this strange earth-creature would stare back at them just as curiously.

The nestlings could not know it, of course, but the sight of them, of their helplessness, was having a marked effect on the farmer.

Like many people he was beginning to realize that the chemicals he was using on his fields were not totally beneficial. He now understood that they were killing a lot of things besides those they were designed to kill. And on top of this he was beginning to have doubts that they would be able to go on doing the job indefinitely.

His insect problem seemed to get worse instead of better. He knew now that many predators were being killed off and that the pests were developing resistant strains. That was why he found himself being forced each year to use more and stronger poisons.

He had to control these insects or he faced ruin. But were chemicals the only answer? He had been studying the matter quite intently. The sight of the baby birds, along with the realization that he might well become their murderer, impelled him to action.

When his mate and the youngsters had had enough food to be at least temporarily and relatively content, Pandion would often perch on top of the pole next to the one bearing the nest. Here he liked to preen, sun himself, and maintain a vigil over his family and the surrounding countryside.

From this vantage point he was accustomed to seeing the farmer walking through his fields. Usually the man went empty-handed, stopping every now and then to examine the young stems and leaves of his plants. But one morning Pandion saw him entering the field holding a large object on his shoulder.

It was a basket and every now and then the farmer would stop and open it, releasing a swarm of flying insects. Some swallows and a kingbird who was starting a nest in the yard were following the man, trying to pick off some of the insects. In this the birds were seldom successful since the insects were quick to swoop down into the cover of the corn plants.

Pandion was uninterested. Like the falcon he had sometimes played at chasing insects in the air, but he did not want to eat the tiny creatures as did the swallows and the kingbird, so all this did not seem to concern him.

Here he was wrong. It concerned him vitally. Or it would have concerned him if what the farmer was trying to do could have been successful.

What the farmer had been studying were reports of various "natural" or "biological" methods of controlling insect pests that scientists were trying to develop as possible substitutes for chemicals.

The oldest of these, which men had been using for more than a hundred years, was simply to set loose some natural predator and hope that they would devour the pests. To this end, the farmer was releasing some ladybugs in his fields.

He was under no illusion that this alone would do the job. He only hoped that less poison might have to be used if he could restore the upset ecological balance by reinforcing the depleted ranks of the predators.

He was doing this on his own, for he had received no encouragement from the experts. He had checked with the agricultural authorities, federal and state, whose advice he had taken in the past. Their offices were full of pamphlets on the latest chemical pesticides. They had little or nothing on natural control methods.

They tended to be skeptical of the entire idea. They insisted, rightly, that as far as present knowledge went, these controls would not be nearly as effective as chemicals. They indicated that natural methods were used mainly by crackpot conservationists, faddists, or dilettantes, not by serious professional farmers.

He got the same reactions from the people at the crop-dusting service and from the salesmen sent out by the chemical companies. These men were trained experts, too, armed with detailed factual knowledge of the concoctions (manufactured by their companies) that would be most effective in meeting each insect problem. None had an encouraging word for any other kind of control.

Nevertheless the farmer decided to try an alternative method. He studied reports of experiments in the sterilization and release of male pest insects. In some cases this had reduced populations. He also read how artificial sexual attractants had been developed that had also, experimentally at least, served to reduce insect populations. There were other nonchemical controls under study, such as spreading diseases or genetic defects among the pests.

The use of predators seemed the most promising and practical so he ordered the ladybugs from a west-coast firm.

Ladybugs, or lady beetles, have for a long time been known to be beneficial to man. Their name goes back to feudal times when they were dedicated to the Virgin Mary and were called "Beetles of Our Lady."

Some species, when the cold weather approaches, congregate in vast swarms, usually in mountainous areas. Here they are collected, some say "by the ton," and put in cold storage for the winter. They are then sold to amateur gardeners and sometimes to farmers, for release in the spring.

Their favorite food is aphids. In fact, one would think nothing could relish aphids as much as an adult ladybug. But after they deposit their eggs on the undersides of leaves and the young caterpillarlike larvae emerge, these youngsters will start eating even more aphids than their parents.

After releasing the ladybugs there was nothing for the farmer to do but wait and see if these speckled little beetles and their progeny would do their work. He was never going to know.

A few days later, just after Pandion had brought a fish into the nest, the birds were disturbed by the roar of an airplane. They were, of course, accustomed to these huge noisy things in the air and usually paid them little attention.

But this one was flying very low, scarcely higher than the nest on the pole, and was headed directly toward the ospreys. One of the young birds, in his eagerness for the food Pandion had brought in, had climbed up on the edge of the nest. The roar of the plane drowned out any warning cries the old birds might have given.

It passed only a few feet above them. Had Nassa not done her construction work well, the entire nest would have been blown to pieces. As it was, both the old birds and the youngster on the edge were blown off the platform.

Nassa and Pandion managed to right themselves and, with flapping wings, remain safely in the air. The youngster, unable yet to fly, fell to the ground.

Now the screams of alarm of both parent birds could be heard in the house. The farmer had come running out at the noise of the plane. If he heard the birds he paid no attention. He was watching the plane. It had passed over his fields and was now crisscrossing over those of the neighbor.

The pilot had opened his valves and the poisoned mist was settling over the young plants. But not all of it. There was a breeze that was carrying much of the excess, the 50 percent that goes beyond the immediate target, over the farmer's fields.

The insects that had been feeding on his neighbor's plantings—and the insect predators that had been feeding on them—were falling in spastic deaths. And, as the mist drifted inexorably over his fields, so were the farmer's lady-bugs.

The kingbirds, the swallows, and the other insect eaters were feasting on the dying. Eventually they, too, would go into convulsions.

The farmer's attention was now diverted to the ospreys. Pandion and Nassa were diving and screaming at a cat at the foot of their pole. Just as the farmer looked he saw the cat running off with the struggling youngster who had been blown from the nest. There was no chance of stopping him.

The man looked up at the one remaining baby peering out of the nest. He resolved he would not give up.

Next day the farmer started talking to his neighbors. It was obvious that if natural controls were going to have any chance at all they would have to be applied on a wider basis than one man's farm. He pleaded for the others to join him. But they quoted the experts: Only chemicals were effective; other methods lay in the distant and improbable future.

In vain did the farmer plead that by the time the distant future arrived the whole earth might be poisoned. Let the whole earth then cooperate, said the others. Not just us. We are not the only ones poisoning the earth. What about industrial wastes? Air pollution? What about oil spillages? Mercury poisoning? Thermal pollution?

And, they asked, if our crops are not free of insect harm, how can we compete with those that are. We'll stop using chemicals when everyone else does, when people are willing to go back to buying fruit with worms in it, or corn partly eaten by caterpillars.

But then one farmer proposed a compromise. They were all still using DDT or some of its relatives, long-lasting poisons that remained in the environment for a good many years. There were now some other insecticides on the market, just as potent or even more so, but without such a long-term effect. Why not try them?

The farmers discussed this with representatives of the chemical firms that produced these alternative poisons. They had a great deal of accurate data on just which variety was best for each specific crop and pest. They advised the farmers that it would be wise for them to start using these new chemicals anyway for they might all of a sudden be compelled to do so.

The public outcry against DDT, they conceded, was such that it might soon be banned in all the states. They assured the farmers their new products were just as strong. They would do the job. They just would not last as long.

The crop duster was a little more honest. These farmers were friends of his. If the shift to less long-lived chemicals was made, he pointed out, they would simply have to be used more often.

This would be fine for his business, and the chemical companies would make greater profits, but it would be more expensive for the farmers. In the end the farmers decided to switch to the new chemicals anyway.

So Pandion and Nassa and their one remaining youngster began seeing the great noisy creature flying and belching over the fields quite often. They did not fear it, but the fumes it emitted were offensive to them so, whenever the wind blew the effusions over the nest, they would fly up and circle about or go find a perching place away from it until the mist subsided.

They could do this because their offspring was now old enough so he did not require constant attention. But he could not leave the nest.

When the fumes were so bad that his parents went away, the farmer and his family usually stayed in their house with the doors closed. The young osprey, perforce, had to stay in the open and assimilate the noxious air.

He was not the only one. In the past, with many fewer sprayings, the air in this rural area, if not the water and the earth and the inhabitants, was usually free of poisons. Eating rather than breathing, was the dangerous activity.

Then, too, in the past when different farmers wanted sprayings at different times, the duster would cover a relatively small area. Many creatures would flee into neighboring, uncontaminated fields to get away from the fumes. Now, for many, this was not possible.

Many birds, except those that stayed to feed on dying insects or other creatures, still did get away on their wings. But others could only run or crawl from one field to another and this was often not far enough to escape the fumes.

After the dustings, the farmer walked through his fields, now with a heavy heart. The insects that had been threatening his crops were under control. This he liked. But there were many things he did not like. The poison was building up in the bodies of mammals as well as other animals.

He found a squirrel rigid in death, his back bowed, the toes of his feet tightly clenched, his mouth full of dirt from biting the earth in his last agonies. There was a field mouse, still alive, lying on its back in convulsions, unable to right itself.

He saw a group of a neighbor's sheep bleating continuously, staggering as though intoxicated, struggling to get to a small pond to quench an overpowering thirst. Two managed to drink and die before the neighbor came running to herd them to a barn.

Even mammals that could, for protection, get into barns —or houses—were not entirely spared.

The farmer read the warnings that came with the insecticides and heeded them. Some others did not. Newspapers carried reports of farm workers reentering fields too soon and paying for their carelessness with their lives.

The crop duster was an experienced man and brought home to his assistants the hazards of their occupation and the cautions they must use. Others were not so careful.

A man in a hangar, washing out the tanks of a spray plane, doused himself. He died. A pilot in a plane with a leaky valve inhaled some of the fumes. He crashed and died.

And men found other, ingenious ways to use these pesticides. Quite a few despondents killed themselves with these poisons, and at least one used such a substance for murder.

❧ 13 ❧

It was now time for the one remaining youngster of Pandion and Nassa to start trying his wings, but it was becoming obvious he would never be able to do so.

Perhaps his brother, who was blown from the nest by the plane, was the lucky one. His death had been relatively fast and painless. This final survivor was simply wasting away. He ate less and less of the food Pandion continued to bring in although Nassa tore it into small pieces for him. Finally he became too weak to eat at all.

At first the puzzled parents ate the food themselves but soon Pandion stopped bringing his catches to the nest and Nassa began leaving the youngster more often to fish for herself. There were no commands of nature bidding them bring food to an offspring who refused it.

When his parents were away the young osprey did not remain motionless, frozen as he should. He could not. The poisons he had inhaled, working on his nervous system, were bringing on tremors and convulsions. These movements in the nest, violent twitchings and shudders, were sure to catch the eye of a predator.

It was a crow, flying overhead, who was first attracted. Pandion and Nassa were both away at the time so the crow dipped down to investigate. Faced with this threat the young osprey summoned his fading strength and lunged at the invader. At that point the crow discovered that he did not have a small nestling to deal with but a bird almost as large as himself. He flew away.

But the young osprey's respite was brief. That evening, just before dusk when Pandion and Nassa were again away from the nest, a more formidable enemy came by. A great horned owl, starting his nightly hunt, caught sight of motion in the nest. Down he came and without trouble carried the struggling bird away.

In the end the young osprey would have his revenge. The flesh on which the owl feasted had enough poison to ensure that.

Pandion and Nassa stayed around the nest for several weeks even though their last youngster was gone. As summer began turning into fall, however, they started wandering, sometimes together, sometimes alone.

They were together on the Susquehanna River north of the headwaters of the bay when the first cold snap came. Pandion remembered his flight south and headed inland toward Hawk Mountain.

There was no command to maintain the pair bond now that the nesting season was over. Had there been other ospreys around Nassa might have stayed with them for she had spent her life on the eastern seaboard. But it had been weeks since she had seen another osprey. Out of Pandion's sight she felt lonely. She followed him.

Pandion led her to the mountains. Without difficulty he

found an updraft and the two started the rising, soaring, coasting trip to the south. The air currents were just as Pandion had experienced them before. In fact everything seemed the same with one big exception.

On the earlier trip he had been surrounded by other members of the great order of hawks, scores of them traveling with him. Now he saw only an occasional bird. For the most part the skies over the mountains were empty.

On his earlier trip Pandion had also seen many smaller birds busily heading south. These were mostly warblers, vireos, and other migrants. There were still quite a few of these birds but every now and then Pandion would see one suddenly fold its wings and drop to the ground.

Before setting forth on this long journey these little birds had had to build up their fat. They had been feeding heavily on poisoned insects in poisoned forests. For many, when they began drawing on this fat, the poison entering the rest of their body was fatal.

This did not concern Pandion as he and Nassa flew on to the Gulf of Mexico. Here they fished and worked their way south until they arrived at the broad estuary where Pandion had made his headquarters during his previous stay in Florida.

Here he settled down again and while he paid no attention to Nassa and she very little to him they were usually within sight of one another. The fish seemed a little livelier and harder to catch and there were not so many of them but the ospreys managed to get enough.

The birds were seldom bothered now by the low-flying, belching planes. For a great change had taken place here in the short time since Pandion had left. Instead of airplanes laying their noxious mists over the marshes, Pandion often saw beneath him large earthbound machines. They were draglines and other heavy equipment with which men were digging canals and constructing dikes.

The men were eliminating isolated pools of water. In previous years when such pools had gone dry, mosquitoes had laid eggs in the mud or sand. When the waters rose with the summer rains the eggs had hatched. Myriads of wrigglers would pupate and mosquitoes would swarm over the land, for the wrigglers were free of their principal enemy, little fish.

Now, the isolated pools having been eliminated by connecting canals, minnows could get into them and feed on the wrigglers. Here, indeed, was a "biological control." And it was working. Men in effect were introducing a natural predator by making sure minnows could feast on their favorite prey—mosquito larvae.

Pandion and Nassa and others like them had not suddenly found an uncontaminated oasis. It was only a start.

Factories up the rivers still dumped their wastes into the streams, and inland farmers, who needed to control many insects besides mosquitoes, continued to use chemical poisons that found their way into the earth, air, and water.

An aroused public was now trying to bring some measure of control to some of this wantonness. But just as the farmer on the Chesapeake could not do it on one farm, this public effort would be largely futile in one country or even on one continent.

Across the gulf from Pandion was Mexico, and to the south lay Central America and the great continent of South America with its exploding populations. All through this area many men in many countries in many ways were applying DDT or some of its relatives to their lands.

Across the Atlantic was Africa with its burgeoning nations and here, too, lands were being doused with chemicals. And across the Pacific was teeming Asia where men had also found that these new and cheap chemicals were offering solutions to age-old problems.

Representatives of many of these countries had had meetings with worried scientists at the United Nations in New York. Suggestions that the use of some of these chemicals be slowed down or controlled were greeted coldly.

"The insecticides in many places have just about eliminated malaria, typhus, sleeping sickness, and other diseases that used to kill thousands," said one diplomat at one such meeting. "Do you expect us now to tell our people they can no longer be used?"

"Our food production is up by forty percent as a result of these insecticides," said another. "Thousands who used to starve are now being saved."

"We now have a chance at some of the good things of life you in the rich nations have had for years," said a third. "We will never give up DDT."

And so poisons continued to be applied to much of the earth's atmosphere and surface. And from these spots of deliberate contamination, it continued to be diffused to many others.

Winds carried it to the poles and around the equator. Streams carried it to rivers, which carried it to estuaries. Ocean currents carried it throughout the seas. Migratory birds carried it across the oceans. Fish and other aquatic animals carried it throughout their realms.

Amid the ice floes in the Arctic Circle in northern Spitzbergen a polar bear had for some time found fishing easier than usual. His prey seemed less wary and elusive. He had fed well. Now he lay on the ice, sick and listless.

On another ice island at the other end of the earth, in the Antarctic, a male penguin was incubating the single egg his mate had left with him. His ability to keep this egg warm and nurture the life within at outside temperatures as low as seventy degrees below zero is one of nature's triumphs. To do so, the father penguin held the egg on the top of his foot, pressing over it a fold of warm skin and feathers.

This he had been doing without interruption for eight weeks, during which he had not been able to eat and had lost a third of his weight. The egg should now be hatching but it was never going to. It was sterile. Soon the penguin would abandon it, but he was doomed himself. He had been living on his fat for too long.

❧ 14 ❧

The ospreys stayed in Florida until the spring bade them head north. Pandion left first and was followed in a few days by Nassa, who joined him at the nesting area.

The nest was still on the pole and needed only minor repairs which, after the usual courting ceremonies, the two ospreys set about making.

The farmer noted the return of the birds with misgivings. The land, he knew, and the air and the water were as heavily poisoned as ever. Walking through his fields he found many dead birds and mammals. Once he had watched a demented mother rabbit eat her own babies. If he had to witness many more such scenes he felt he would have to sell his farm and try to find some other occupation.

Perry, the falcon, did not return to the area at all. The urges that in the past had always brought him back to his nesting area were no longer working within him. He wandered a bit along the Atlantic coast and finally flew out over the ocean. He was not seen again.

Baldy had returned to his nesting tree but on the way his mate had faltered in her flight until one morning when they were almost home she folded her wings and dropped from the air, dead.

For Baldy, whose normal desires had been getting steadily weaker anyway, this put an end to them altogether. He remained in the area but never again would he try to find a mate. Although the eagle would live for some time, the chemicals he had ingested had already disrupted the complicated physical processes necessary for successful bird reproduction.

This disruption could take a variety of forms. It was now about to be visited on Nassa as she and Pandion prepared once more to try to raise a family.

External stimuli, warmer, and longer days, brought about at first the normal responses in Nassa. In parts of her brain hormones were produced that were responsible for many things: for the territorial urge, the response to courtship, the activation of sex organs, the desire to mate, the production of eggs and the delivery of stored-up calcium to the oviduct to form the shells.

Some of the poison Nassa had been accumulating was lodged in her liver. Here it was bringing about a curious reaction. Certain enzymes were being produced that would attack the sex hormones inhibiting their production in sufficient amount for normal sexual development and behavior.

Depending on the extent and nature of this attack, almost any aberration might be produced. Nassa would respond to Pandion's courtship, but her egg laying was late and the eggs had almost no shells at all, only the inner membrane.

Nevertheless, Nassa still had the compulsion to incubate them. But when she pressed her body down on the eggs they collapsed.

[137]

The farmer did not know of this tragedy. Both birds stayed around the nest and he thought they were just a little late this year. He again started stocking his pool with fish to help Pandion.

Sometimes, when he had enough, the farmer would eat some of the larger fish himself. The ospreys on the nesting pole had often watched him preparing his fish, a preparation that, perhaps, was saving him from the fate overtaking the birds.

The day after Nassa's eggs were broken she was standing by the nest watching the farmer clean a fish on the dock. He did not eat all the fish as the birds did. He carefully cut away and discarded most of the fatty tissue that contained the greatest accumulation of poison.

Ordinarily Nassa would not eat anything except fish that had been caught live by herself or by Pandion. But now the poisons in her body were working their way into her nervous system. This could be responsible for many kinds of abnormal behavior.

She swooped down to the inlet and picked up a floating strip of fat thrown out by the farmer. The man watched her curiously as she returned to the pole and gulped it down. This was going to raise the toxicity in her body beyond any tolerance.

The next morning when Pandion went off to fish, Nassa failed to follow him. When the farmer came out of the house she remembered the food of the day before and flew toward him. She did not get that far.

Her wings suddenly drooped. She fell to the ground almost

[138]

at the farmer's feet. She twitched spasmodically, clutched at the air with her talons, and died.

The farmer did not touch her. He walked slowly back into his house.

Pandion returned in a few hours. Puzzled, he flew about looking for his mate. When he failed to find her he took off toward the bay.

For several days Pandion wandered along the shores, roosting wherever he happened to be at night. It was aimless. He was not seeking another mate. It would have done little good if he had found one.

Within his body foreign enzymes also had been produced. In his case they had rendered him sterile. Never again would he produce living sperm.

Finally he came back to the nesting site and perched on the pole by the now deserted nest. There was no sign of the farmer or his wife. It was a windy day and Pandion felt unsteady.

Below him he could see that a new structure had been erected in front of the house. Pandion was tired—he tired easily now—and he thought this might be a better resting place. He flew down and perched on the lower structure, which was more protected from the wind.

He was resting, swaying slightly, on a sign that read: "Farm for Sale."

NOTE ON SOURCES

No one is responsible for anything in this book besides myself but I do wish to express my gratitude to some.

My wife, Jane Eads Bancroft, was encouraging and helpful throughout and her many suggestions all proved valuable. I would also like to thank fellow naturalists and field companions Mr. and Mrs. Hal H. Harrison for reading the manuscript, making suggestions, and catching errors.

Research Biologist Lawrence J. Blus and his fellow scientists at Patuxent Wildlife Research Center, Maryland, were unfailingly cooperative with this poor layman and, finally, my thanks to the constructive crop duster with a heart, Al Johnson of Magnolia, Delaware, for explaining the secrets of his trade.

This is a work of fiction but, I hope, scientifically accurate fiction. So, for those who might question or, hopefully, for those who might wish to pursue these matters further, I have listed a few of the many writings I found most useful.

Books on Pescides

Carson, Rachel. *Silent Spring*. Boston: Houghton Mifflin, 1962. (This is as timely as when it was first written and is well worth rereading.)

Graham, Frank, Jr. *Since Silent Spring*. Boston: Houghton Mifflin, 1970. (A valuable summary of recent findings that rightly emphasizes what has NOT happened since *Silent Spring*.)

Hickey, Joseph J., ed. *Peregrine Falcon Populations*. Madison, Wisc.: University of Wisconsin Press, 1969. (An excellent symposium of reports from many countries on the use and effect of pesticides.)

Marx, Wesley. *The Frail Ocean*. New York: Ballantine Books, 1969. (A good popular account of many kinds of pollution.)

Miller, Morton, and Berg, George G., eds. *Chemical Fallout*. Springfield, Ill.: Chas. C. Thomas, 1969. (A collection of twenty-five scientific reports that cover a wide field from the First Rochester Conference on Toxicity.)

Moore, N. W., ed. *Journal of Applied Ecology* 3: Supplement. Oxford, England: Blackwell Scientific Publications, 1966. (Another valuable collection of scientific reports.)

Rienow, Robert, and Train, Leona. *Moment in the Sun*. New York: Ballantine Books, 1969. (Excellent account of many phases of man-made problems.)

Rudd, Robert L. *Pesticides and the Living Landscape*. Madison, Wisc.: University of Wisconsin Press, 1964. (This is a storehouse of material valuable to the casual reader and the researcher and covers almost all aspects of the problem.)

United States Government Publications
Washington, D.C.: Government Printing Office

Fish & Wildlife Service Circular 167. *Pesticide Wildlife Studies*, 1963.

————. Circular 226. *Effects of Pesticides on Fish and Wildlife*, 1965.

————. Special Scientific Report-Wildlife 119. *Organochlorine Pesticides in the Environment*, 1968. (Excellent comprehensive summary by Dr. Lucille F. Stickel.)

President's Scientific Advisory Commission. *Restoring the Quality of Our Environment*, 1965.

U.S. Congress, Senate. *Pesticides and Public Policy: Report No. 1379*, 89th Cong., 2d sess., 1966.

Pesticides: General Articles

Atkins, T. D., and Linder, R. L., "Effects of Dieldrin on Reproduction of Penned Hen Pheasants." *Journal of Wildlife Management* 31 (1967): 746–53.

Boykins, Ernest A. "DDT Residues in the Food Chain of Birds." *Atlantic Naturalist* 21 (1966): 18–25.

Breijer, C. J. "The Growing Resistance of Insects to Insecticides." *Atlantic Naturalist* 13 (1958): 149–55.

Cornwall, George. "Environmental Hazards of Pesticides." *Florida Naturalist* 44 (1971). (A timely summary with a valuable bibliography.)

Davis, Kenneth S. "The Deadly Dust." *American Heritage* 22 (1971): 44*ff*. (A good history of DDT.)

DeWitt, James B. "Effects of Chemical Sprays on Wildlife."
Audubon Magazine 60 (1958): 68–70.

Ehrlich, Paul R. "People Pollution." *Audubon Magazine* 72
(1970): 68–70. (Dangers of monoculture and killing predators.)

Graber, Richard R., et al. "Effects of a Low-level Dieldrin
Application on a Red-winged Blackbird Population." *Wilson Bulletin* 77 (1965): 168–74. (Reactions from aberra-
tions to death.)

Harrington, Robert Q., Jr., and Bidlingmayer, W. L. "Effects
of Dieldrin on Fishes and Invertebrates of a Salt Marsh."
Journal of Wildlife Management 22 (1958): 76–82.

Hickey, Joseph J. "DDT and Birds in Wisconsin." *Atlantic
Naturalist* 24 (1969): 86–92. (Good account of physiological effects.)

Jeffries, D. J. "The Delay in Ovulation Produced by DDT."
Ibis 109 (1967): 266–72.

Mills, Herbert R. "Death in the Florida Marshes." *Audubon
Magazine* 54 (1952): 285–91. (A vivid description—ten
years before Rachel Carson!)

Odum, Eugene P. "Lipid Deposition in Nocturnal Migrant
Birds." *Proceedings Twelfth International Ornithological
Congress*, 1960, pp. 563–75. (Storing up and drawing on
fat.)

Peakall, David B. "How Insects Resist Insecticides." *Audubon Magazine* 66 (1964): 32–33.

———. "Pesticides and the Reproduction of Birds." *Scientific American* 219 (1970): 72–78. (These two articles
give detailed explanation of hormonal inhibition.)

———. "Progress in Experiments on the Relation between

Pesticides and Fertility." *Atlantic Naturalist* 22 (1967): 108–11.

Risebrough, R. W. "DDT Residues in Pacific Seabirds." *Nature* 216 (1967): 589–91.

———. "Pesticides: Transatlantic Movements in N.E. Trades." *Science* 159 (1968): 1233–36. (These articles stress diffusion.)

Scott, T. G., et al. "Some Effects of Dieldrin on Wildlife." *Journal of Wildlife Management* 23 (1959): 409–27. (Description of death throes of birds, sheep, and others.)

Spencer, Steven M. "Fighting Insects with Insects." *National Wildlife* 9 (1971): 48–51.

Stickel, William H., et al. "Body Condition and Response to Pesticides in Woodcocks." *Journal of Wildlife Management* 29 (1965): 147–55.

———. "Effects of Heptachlor Contaminated Earthworms on Woodcocks." *Journal of Wildlife Management* 29 (1965): 132–46. (Vivid description of woodcock deaths.)

Woodwell, George M. "Toxic Substances and Ecological Cycle." *Scientific American* 216 (1967): 24–31. (Worldwide diffusion.)

Wurster, Charles, Jr. "DDT Reduces Photosynthesis by Marine Phytoplankton." *Science* 159 (1968): 1474–75.

Pesticides and Birds of Prey

Ames, Peter L., and Mersereau, G. S. "Some Factors in the Decline of the Osprey in Connecticut." *Auk* 81 (1964): 173–85.

[145]

Cade, Tom J., et al. "Peregrines and Pesticides in Alaska." *Condor* 70 (1968): 170–78.

Chura, Nicholas, and Stewart, Paul. "Care, Food Consumption and Behavior of Bald Eagles used in DDT Tests." *Wilson Bulletin* 76 (1967): 441–48.

Dewitt, James, and Buckley, John L. "Studies in Pesticide–Eagle Relationships." *Audubon Field Notes* 16 (1962): 541.

Enderson, J. H. "Breeding and Migration Survey of the Peregrine Falcon." *Wilson Bulletin* 77 (1965): 327–39.

———, and Berger, D. D. "Chlorinated Hydrocarbon Residues in Peregrine and Prey." *Condor* 70 (1968): 149–53.

Henny, Charles J., and Wight, H. M. "An Endangered Osprey Population." *Auk* 86 (1969): 188–98.

Hess, John. "Where Have All the Ospreys Gone?" *National Wildlife* 9 (1971): 36–37.

Locke, Louis N., et al. "Spermatogenisis in Bald Eagles Experimentally Fed DDT." *Condor* 68 (1966): 497–502.

Ott, George. "Is the Bald Eagle Doomed?" *National Wildlife* 8 (1970): 4–9.

Ratcliffe, D. A. "Broken Eggs in Peregrine Eyries." *British Birds* 51 (1958): 23–26.

———. "Decrease in Egg Shell Weight in Certain Birds of Prey." *Nature* 215 (1967): 208–10. (Tells of birds eating their own eggs.)

———. "The Peregrine Situation in Great Britain." *Bird Study* 14 (1967): 238–46.

Reese, Jan. G. "Reproduction in a Chesapeake Bay Osprey Population." *Auk* 87 (1970): 747–59.

Reichel, W. L., et al. "Residues in Two Bald Eagles Suspected of Pesticide Poisoning." *Bulletin of Environmental*

Contamination and Toxicology 4 (1969): 24–30. (Falling dead from air.)

Birds of Prey: Books

Abbott, Clinton. *The Home Life of the Osprey*. London: Witherby, 1911.

Abbott, Jacob Bates. *Birds of Prey of Eastern United States*. New Brunswick, N.J.: Rutgers University Press, 1948.

Baker, J. A. *The Peregrine*. New York: Harper & Row, 1967. (Detailed and absorbing account of peregrines in England.)

Bent, Arthur Cleveland. *Life Histories of North American Birds of Prey*. 2 vols. Washington, D.C.: U.S. National Museum, 1937. (Bent's classics are still unsurpassed in their field.)

Brown, Leslie, and Amadon, Dean. *Eagles Hawks and Falcons of the World*. 2 vols. Feltham, Middlesex, England: Country Life Books, 1968. (The latest, biggest, and most expensive.)

Grossman, M. L., and Hamlet, John. *Birds of Prey of the World*. N.Y.: Bonanza Books, 1964. (Second only to the above.)

Hausman, Leon A. *Birds of Prey of Northeastern North America*. New Brunswick, N.J.: Rutgers University Press, 1948.

Herrick, Francis H. *The American Eagle*. N.Y.: Appleton-Century, 1934.

Mannix, Dan. *The Last Eagle*. N.Y.: McGraw-Hill, 1965.

(Good, scientifically accurate fiction.)

Murphy, Robert. *The Peregrine Falcon.* Boston: Houghton Mifflin, 1964. (Also good, scientifically accurate fiction.)

Sprunt, Alexander, Jr. *North American Birds of Prey.* N.Y.: Bonanza Books, 1965.

Birds of Prey: Articles

Allen, Charles Stover. "Breeding Habits of the Fishhawk on Plum Island, N.Y." *Auk* 9 (1892): 313–21.

Ames, Peter L. "Notes on Nesting Behavior of the Osprey." *Atlantic Naturalist* 19 (1964): 15–27.

Beebe, Frank L. "The Marine Peregrines of the NW Pacific Coast." *Condor* 62 (1960): 145–89.

Cade, Tom J. "Ecology of the Peregrine and Gyrfalcon in Alaska." *University of California Publications in Zoology* 63 (1960): 151–290.

Fullerton, George J. "Bald Eagle Captures Duck." *Loon* 41 (1969): 27.

Heintzelman, Donald S. "Wings over Hawk Mountain." *National Wildlife* 8 (1970): 22–27.

Herbert, R. A., and K. G. S. "Behavior of Peregrine Falcons in the New York City Area." *Auk* 82 (1965): 62–94.

Knight, C. W. R. "Photographing the Nest of the Osprey." *National Geographic* 62 (1932): 247–60.

Meinertzhagen, R. "The Education of Young Ospreys." *Ibis* 96 (1954): 153–55.

Nickell, Walter P. "Breast-wetting Behavior of the Osprey at the Nest." *Jack Pine Warbler* 45 (1967): 96–97.

Postupalsky, Serge, and Kleiman, Joseph P. "Osprey Preys on Turtle." *Wilson Bulletin* 77 (1965): 401–2.

Sindelar, Charles, and Schluter, Errol. "Osprey Carrying Bird." *Wilson Bulletin* 80 (1968): 103.

Storer, John H. "The Flight of Birds." *Cranbrook Institute of Science Bulletin* 28, 1948.